SPECTATOR

SPECTATOR

A NOVEL BY RACHEL SALAZAR

FICTION COLLECTIVE   NEW YORK · BOULDER

First Edition

Library of Congress Cataloging in Publication Data

Salazar, Rachel.
    Spectator.

I. Title.
PS3569.A459S64   1986   813.'54   86-4477
ISBN: 0-932-51104-X
ISBN: 0-932-51105-8 (pbk.)

Published by Fiction Collective with assistance from the National
Endowment for the Arts; the support of the Publications Center,
University of Colorado, Boulder; and with the cooperation of Brooklyn
College, Illinois State University and Teachers & Writers
Collaborative.

Grateful acknowledgment is also made to the Graduate School, the
School of Arts and Sciences, and the President's Fund of the University
of Colorado, Boulder.

The author wishes to thank Creative Artists Public Service Program for
the grant received.

Thanks also to Jonathan Baumbach and Peter Spielberg for much time
and encouragement.

Typeset by Fisher Composition, Inc.

Manufactured in the United States of America

Designed by Abe Lerner

For Lenny and Jeanne

Contents

SPECTATOR

THE STREET

This street is the most direct way to the supermarket, the park, the laundromat, the movie theater, the bank, the bakery. Mara counts how many steps it takes to cover a square of pavement, a half-block, a block. The light changes to red. She waits at the corner.

A man—tall, thin, wearing a leather jacket, his dark hair cropped—will be walking toward her, walking aggressively, shoulders moving forward, head level.

She will keep her eyes on him, ready to avert them when he comes near enough. When he stops before her, she will pretend that she has just seen him. He'll be friendly. Surely, he will. But how should she be? Will she assume a hurt expression, or should she try to charm him? "Everything is hunky-dory." He won't even know what that means. What will he say? "Do you have a lover?" Will she lie, or tell the truth? Does it matter?

The man will come into focus, but it won't be Rafael—the body too wide, the legs too thick, the shoulders sloped, the neck too long. This man will be taller, older, bald.

He will say hello.

She will be cautious. "I thought you were someone else, someone I know."

"But we do know each other."

She will not recognize him immediately.

"We met a few years ago."

She will then remember the thin lips, the even bar of false teeth. "You look different." She will not want to talk to him, but will say his name aloud to herself, so that she will not forget it next time.

He will smile, as if he is amused by her uncertainty. "I live in the same place. Come to visit sometime." He will bend down. "You don't mind?"

She will shake her head as she allows him to kiss her.

The light turns green.

12

THE MEETING

Under a lamp, Mara and Hildy and the two men, Rafael and Ascencio, sat around a wooden table.

Mara would rather have been with someone else.

Hildy's flat was white, spare, straight lines up to the ceilings, no moldings.

Hildy was curved, had long calves.

She kept an acropolis in a bottle.

Her china was white and plain, the silver polished.

Mara lifted her knife and rubbed its smooth handle, then reached for her glass.

Rafael was watching her. She had just met him. The edge of her glass had a faint lipstick mark, which

13

must have been hers. She touched her lip. Some red came off on her finger. He looked from mouth to finger. The gesture observed, she smiled, a little embarrassed.

Everyone was there. No one saw what happened.

Did you talk to her?

Impossible . . . so many people . . .

He kept shooting?

No film in the camera. Nobody noticed till everyone had left.

Rafael had a skull face, high cheekbones over hollow cheeks. The whites of his eyes were muddy. He said little. When he spoke, his low voice was surprising. He had a heavy accent, pronounced carefully, but the words came out thick and indistinct, as if his tongue got in the way.

When Hildy stood, he watched her without seeming to.

She returned, carrying a celadon serving dish, set it down, uncovered it—inside, rosy tentacles, big fan-shaped mushrooms, ruffled black fungi.

Hildy's slanted eyes made it hard to tell what she was thinking. Her fuzzy sweater obscured the line of her shoulder. "If you cook it too long, it loses its tenderness." She lit a cigarette, leaned back in her chair, tilted her head, inhaled.

Ascencio, cocking one eyebrow, shook his head and stamped his feet. His face made Mara tired.

She preferred the bodies to the squirming arms.

14

THE MEETING

The mushrooms tasted of earth. Wiping the corners
of her mouth, she caught Rafael staring at her again.
She stared back. He dropped his eyes—looked away,
laughed, showing big white teeth, spit a little when
he laughed.

*He followed her . . . never spoke . . . She remembered
later . . .*

She wore black?

Couldn't stop talking about it.

Her glass was empty. Rafael, speaking slowly,
poured more wine. His fingers were brown and
stubby. He did it so slowly. She held her glass for a
very long time, then felt the stem slipping, almost
let go. The wine smelled fruity, but, as she sipped,
she found it had no taste.

Fifty-thousand dollars. The dealer got fifty percent.

Better not to sell at all.

"Tired?" Hildy put her hand on Mara's shoulder.

She shook her head, whispered. Both men stopped
talking, as if they wanted to hear what the women
were saying.

Mara rested her chin on one hand, playing with her
hair, laid her knife across her plate, examined the
hem of the tablecloth, noticing the stitches.

Ascencio took the cord with a charm from his neck
and passed it to her. "It's crystal." The quartz was
warm, milky rather than clear, had been carved into a
skull, its sockets set with green sparkling stones.

"Paste?" Mara asked.

15

"Emeralds." He pulled his forked beard, rocked back in his chair.

She passed the skull to Hildy. "Why is it cloudy?"

After melon cakes and squares of rice paste, Mara brushed the crumbs from the tablecloth. She had almost forgotten that she would rather have been with someone else. The kettle whistled. Mara measured the tea leaves, filled the pot with water, set out the cups.

She opened the door and thought she saw him . . .

Did they fight about it?

She couldn't believe it.

How did it end?

The usual way.

As she poured tea into the cups, she spilled some on the cloth, rushed to the sink to wet a paper towel.

Rafael and Ascencio walked fast, Mara between them.

"I live a few blocks away."

Rafael's smile didn't say anything.

She waited before her building. The zephyr above the door lintel looked angrier than usual.

"Would you like to come up, . . . have a drink?" She heard uncertainty in her own voice.

Ascencio twisted his neck around, said no.

She climbed the stairs. Rafael followed. The marble steps were chipped. They stopped at the third landing.

16

She opened the door and switched on the light. The front room was small and painted white, the only furniture a bed covered by a patchwork quilt and an antique trunk, its metal sides patterned like alligator skin. A hand-painted photograph of a woman in an old-fashioned bathing dress, lifting her skirts and dipping one foot into a pond, hung on an otherwise bare wall.

She folded his jacket, lining out, and laid it on the trunk.

Sitting next to him, but not looking at him, she pulled at the loose threads in the comforter.

"Everything here has been with me a long time."

"All the things look old."

"They came to me old."

"Ascencio says some of us are very old, but I'm young." He held out his hand to her. "See, I have very few lines." He opened his hand.

She bent down and kissed the open palm.

THE WEDDING

Before the priest, Mara and Rafael kneel on the black and white tiles.

Her eyes cast down, as she thinks it is done, she studies the folds in the father's cassock, draped in flutes and columns, one shoe showing—a black, perforated oxford.

Her own dress tucked under her knees does not soften the hardness of the floor. She shifts her weight from one side to the other, tries to balance.

For this cause shall a man leave his father and mother, and cleave to his wife . . .

Rafael clears his throat and looks at her sideways.

18

The back of his neck is very brown above his white shirt collar, his well-shaped ear flat against his skull—the thin cartilage of its upper curve nicked where she cut him. As he lifts his chin, she sees the mole underneath.

Tightening her grip on the bouquet of roses (mostly pink and, oddly, lavender), she jabs her finger on a thorn, which she then breaks off and lets fall. It lands point up.

These roses have a stronger scent than those in the States—sweeter and heavier. The wet leaves still smell of dirt. An ant crawls out of the flushed corolla of a yellow rose, continues onto her finger, then to the back of her hand, her wrist-bone, over the hairs on her arm, then is lost against the black sleeve.

Her head bowed, she raises her eyes. The book presses into the father's belly. A page turns, knuckles crack. His voice keeps its even tone.

Let the husband render unto the wife due benevolence: and likewise also the wife unto the husband.

A baroque style Ascension has been painted on the ceiling above the altar: A pink-skinned, buxom Virgin—eyes gazing heavenward, mouth open in ecstasy, arms uplifted, her drapery swirling about—appears to dance amid a flock of angels hovering in a turquoise sky. A long mottled streak separates the figure's head from its body. Shadows obscure the edges of the fresco.

For it is better to marry than to burn.

19

SPECTATOR

Smelling of soap and coffee, Rafael inclines his head toward her. Their eyes meet. He says something inaudible. His full face, by its coarseness, always surprises and, at the same time, pleases her. His hair is very short like a black cap—a fine, dark aureole around his head. She wants to touch the clipped hair, as one would carefully test the serrated edge of a knife.

Closing her eyes, she concentrates on the darkness inside her eyelids. Her crepe dress suffocates and her skin is damp, palms wet, thighs sticking together. A drop of sweat runs from her armpit down her side. A movement stirs the air; paper rustles. Maybe the priest has turned another page.

And they that weep, as though they wept not; and they that rejoice, as though they rejoiced not . . .

She would like to stand up, to leave, to go back to the house, up to their room, to draw the shade, to take off her dress, her shoes, to lie on the bed, to sleep.

The father's voice slows down, slurring the words of the service. The church becomes quiet.

She is walking with her father in a garden down a path shaded on both sides by cone-shaped trees.

"What garden is this?" she asks.

"Don't you remember?"

"Central Park?"

"No, try again."

A low, early morning fog drifts among the trees in the background.

20

"Hampstead Heath?"

They come to an enclosure hedged by holly bushes. A statue of a woman cast in black metal guards the gate. Mara watches the Kore's blank eyes and parted lips. Dew, like the sweat of passion, coats the sculpture's round arms and breasts.

Her mother, hair in long Cretan ropes, is standing before an open door. She is younger than Mara, maybe nineteen or twenty. Her face is pale, one of her eyebrows much thicker than the other.

Her mother extends a hand to her father.

"Where are we?"

"Versailles."

"Now I remember."

They turn their backs to Mara and, holding hands, enter the doorway. The door bangs behind them.

The book slams closed; she winces. Words are spoken quickly in Spanish. She understands but cannot answer. Rafael stands. She remains on the floor. Reaching down and taking her elbow, he pulls her, gently. She drops the flowers, stoops to pick them up. He shakes his head. She looks at the priest, who shuts his eyes in agreement. Something is done with rings. Rafael's face is enormous as he bends down to kiss her. As he straightens and draws away, his head returns to normal size.

He steadies her arm as they leave the church.

A DAY IN THE COUNTRY

Walking slowly along the path through the cornfields, dragging her sandals over the wet ground,
which gives off a damp warmth, earth rutted by cart
wheels and marked with blurred hoof prints, the
edges of the curving leaves brushing her arms and
legs, Mara falls behind Rafael and Juan, their shiny
black hair like crows' wings among the green stalks.

In the still valley, their voices, though distant, are
clear.

All yours?

*Once my father owned all the land in Amatitlan, but
when he died, my mother sold most of it. . . . Further*

down, by the train station, the fields belong to the village . . .

Everything is green.

It rains each afternoon.

A gust of wind rippling the tufts of corn silk carries the smell of dung and straw as they approach a cattle pen in the clearing ahead.

Rafael stops and calls out to Mara; while Juan, who has gone around behind the pen, comes back dragging a burlap sack.

"Here, put your hands together." He pours some feed into her cupped palms.

"They're so big." She laughs, as she cautiously lifts her hands toward a red and white cow, who lowers her massive head, nuzzling the food that is offered, insects clustering around the wet, brown eyes. The animal's warm saliva spreads over Mara's fingers. She wipes her sticky hands on the back of her shorts. "Is there water around?"

"Only the pond where the cows drink." Juan strokes the cow's ridged back, her head resting on the lower rail of the wooden fence. "You wouldn't want to wash there." He points behind the cow pen to a water hole about fifty feet across, its opaque surface motionless.

Rafael frowns, his lips thrust out in an expression of disgust. "Don't touch it, Mara. It's dirty and you can't see what's in there."

"What is there to see? It must be all right if the

23

SPECTATOR

cows drink it. It's not big—it can't be too deep." She appeals to Juan, who looks back at Rafael.

"It's brown, muddy . . ." His voice is sulky.

"When I was a child, I always swam in muddy lakes. It just means that there's earth on the bottom, not sand or rocks, and that it gets stirred up and comes to the top." She bends over, and unbuckles her sandals, then tests the water with her foot. Although denser than clear water, it feels cool, leaves a brownish mark around her ankle. "Rafael, it's wonderful!"

He crouches on a rock, staring at her.

She pulls off her shorts and dives in, at once immersed in cold, gritty water. She doesn't touch bottom, comes up, is startled as she realizes that the pond is teeming with minnows. Drawing her arm across her mouth, she tastes soil on her skin.

The two men, who are talking, turn to watch her. Rafael throws a pebble that breaks the still water close to her. The minnows dart away, disappearing.

As she swims slowly in a circle, holding her head above water, keeping her mouth closed and breathing through her nose, pushing the silver fish away from her as she parts the water, drawing her legs up to her body, then out and together, she propels herself forward with each kick. The plated back of a turtle surfaces alongside of her, the rotary motion of its legs barely visible.

24

When she reaches the rock on which Juan and Rafael are sitting, she stretches out her hand to lift herself out of the pond. Grabbing her forearm rather roughly, Rafael hauls her up, stomach and thighs scraping against the stones.

"Look at all the fish . . ." The minnows—small, almost transparent, glittering, twitching in the rivulets that run over her skin—cover her body. Dipping her leg into the pond, she tries to wash them away, but only draws out more.

"Water like that is very dangerous." Rafael tosses her shorts at her.

"How?" She tilts her head to one side to drain the water from her ear.

"My father told me stories of people who swam in water where they couldn't see the bottom, and who got tangled up in the underwater plants and drowned. I've heard of animals coming up and dragging people down. You've got to be careful." He wipes something away from her chin.

The outside walls of Juan's house, like the other buildings on the main street, are adobe, stuccoed white, with small, high windows set very close to the roof.

Mara jumps the tall step before the front door, entering a dimly-lit room, apparently a kind of general store, with a counter and shelves stocked with very few items—some boxes of American cereal, disks of Mexican chocolate wrapped in white paper, corn starch, a basket on the counter filled with rolls, and some strings of globular sausages hanging from the ceiling. A box of empty soda bottles stands in the corner.

Following Juan, she passes through another room, unfurnished but with a built-in bench along its walls, out to a covered veranda framing a sunny patio, a dry fountain of smooth gray stone marking its center.

Juan offers them two old chairs, which are placed against the walls of the house, as if the dusty courtyard that they face is some kind of spectacle.

Mara remains standing. "I'd like to look around?"

Glancing at Rafael, who seems not to notice him, Juan hesitates.

"You don't have to come with me. Stay and keep Rafael company."

She walks into the sunshine and across the yard to the opposite side of the quadrangle. Clay roof tiles frame an oblong of sky—uniformly blue, empty of birds and clouds.

An open doorway reveals a small dark room, its walls painted deep rose, the ceiling turquoise. A glossy calendar picturing the black Virgin of Guadalupe hangs like a pinup; a gold chain with a crucifix is looped around one of the nails. Rumpled clothes litter the mattress on the floor. A great many books

26

are stacked into uneven piles, upon one of which sits a small plastic radio with luminous numbers. An empty Delicados package has been crumpled onto a plate filled with half-burned cigarettes. Two neatly executed geometric designs on cheap paper are taped over the window panes, casting small red and yellow reflections over the plastered wall.

She hears the sound of hands clapping from the adjoining section of the house, and, following the noise, comes upon an old woman before a table in a smoky kitchen, a mass of grayish dough before her as she slaps a tortilla between her palms.

The woman, who might be in her eighties, is very wrinkled, and, with her smooth white hair coiled into a bun at the neck, her pale face with round red cheeks and little blue eyes, she does not look Mexican.

Without seeming surprised, she smiles at Mara, baring fleshy, toothless gums. "Too dry," she says in a small voice, punching down a failed tortilla.

Touching the dough, Mara pulls off a piece, which crumbles as she rolls it between her fingers. "Sí, señora. Maybe it needs more water." She tilts the water jug cradled in the metal stand, filling a tin cup, which she passes to the woman, who sprinkles the mound with water.

The next tortilla sticks, and, laughing shrilly, she holds up her palm to show Mara the moist disk clinging to her skin. "Now it's too wet." She peels the

27

dough from her hand and balls it up with a fistful of fresh dough from the pile. The next two are perfect. She begins to work quickly, dipping her fingertips into the water at regular intervals, turning out tortilla after tortilla.

"Ay! the beans." Tapping her forehead, the woman gets up from her chair and grips the table, as if to balance herself. As she holds the edge with one hand, she takes a step toward the stove, and lifts the lid from a large pot, the smell of beans escaping in swirls of steam. With a long-handled wooden spoon, she reaches inside, then scoops out some beans into a clay bowl, which she gives to Mara.

"No, *gracias*. Later."

"I'll bring them to Juan." The old woman turns off the fire under the pot. "Are you a friend of his?"

"Yes."

"Ah, that's good." Wrapping a towel around the pot handles, the woman glances behind her. *"Hijo!"*

Juan, hands shoved deep in his front pockets, leans against the doorway. "Where's lunch?" He sounds impatient. His eyes on the movements of the old woman, he rubs his cheek on his shoulder. "Mara, this is my mother."

She extends her hand to the woman, who turns away, heedless of the gesture.

After Mara has cleared away the empty beer bottles from the folding table on the veranda, she lays out a starched white cloth, plates, and speckled, enameled forks and spoons.

Juan's mother crosses the patio, her muscular bowed legs enclosing an oval between them. She carries a basket, which she sets down, and, uncovering the tortillas, passes them to her son.

"*Señora,* sit down with us." Mara pulls out a chair.

Juan's mother sits, but does not eat. Saying nothing, she seems to listen raptly to the men while she refills an empty plate.

"Your house is very lovely." Mara touches the pebbly stucco behind her. "How long have you lived here?"

Not answering immediately, the old woman, her voice weak, begins to talk. "Always. . . . I was born here. It was my father's home, and, when I married, my husband came to live here with me. I gave birth to my son Juan in that room." She points across the courtyard to the pink room with the blue ceiling. "At that time, flowers grew in the patio—roses and geraniums in pots, purple bougainvilleas climbing the arches to the roof—and the fountain used to run with water all day long." Her voice has gained strength. The hand at her wrinkled throat drops. The fingers play with the lace trim sewn to the bosom of her dress. "My father was a *charro,* and we would have parties with mariachis that started in the afternoons and lasted until morning. . . . I would dance all night long. . . . But the girls are different now.

29

They like to do strange things. Once, Juan brought a Swiss girl to stay with us, and all she wanted to do was drive the tractor through the cornfields. . . . What happened to her, Juan?"

"She went back to Switzerland." His face shines with sweat.

"She was a wonderful girl."

Clouds pass across the blue rectangle of sky, covering it, the light no longer brilliant, no longer bleaching surfaces or sharpening outlines; now its cool grayness softening objects and faces.

"The afternoon rains will come soon." The old woman's round cheeks seem to have lost their color, slackened, falling into jowls that hide the corners of her lips. As she opens her mouth, she places her hand over Mara's, which is resting on the tablecloth. "I've never seen a girl as beautiful as this one."

Rafael smiles from Mara to Juan, who removes his glasses, then tucks them into his shirt pocket. Closing his eyes, he presses the lids tightly together, as if for an instant he is in pain or is trying to hold back tears.

Dark spots spatter the dusty tiles. The old woman lowers her pale eyelashes. "Ay, the rain is here."

In the now even light, her face appears smooth, as if brushed with a fine powder that has filled in the cracks and pores. Her head supported by her small, clenched fist, she appears to be watching a fly as it alights on the table. With a gentle wave of her hand, she fans it away.

Mara looks deeply into her blue eyes, the color like the eyes of a baby or a kitten, which will change within a short time.

The basin of the fountain overflows, water splashing onto the wet floor.

In the silence, the sound of raindrops hitting the clay roof grows louder.

THE WHITE MOUNTAIN

"Is your mother asleep?" Mara puts her arm around Rafael's waist.

She glances over his shoulder. In the twin bed on the other side of the night table, her mother-in-law, Remedios, lies stiffly, arms outside the blankets and hands clasped over her stomach. The curtains are drawn, and the light from the street shines on her face. A pair of polyester pants and a white blouse are folded neatly at the foot of the bed.

"Ay, *Dios!*" Remedios cries out, her hands flying up, then falling down at her sides.

Mara waits, wondering whether her mother-in-law

will wake. Remedios begins breathing regularly again.

Mara smiles at Rafael. He must have seen it, for he pushes her hair away from her eyes.

"Where will we go tomorrow?" She winds her leg around his.

"Monte Alban."

"Will your mother come with us?" She flexes her thigh.

"I think so."

"Is she really interested in the pyramids?"

"No, but we can't leave her in the hotel. She wouldn't go around Oaxaca by herself. Mexican women don't do things like that."

"But if she doesn't care—"

"She wants to go where we go, even if it bores her. . . . It's very hot."

Mara unwraps her leg, pushing the blanket away but leaving the already damp sheet over them. She looks again at Remedios, whose face is even more peevish in sleep without her smile or her giggle to sweeten the sour mouth. With surprise, Mara wonders how those small, angry features and heavy jowls have been pleasingly translated into Rafael's face. Will his eyes and nose eventually sink into his cheeks, and his jaws come to hang about his neck?

She gets up and walks to the window. From the second floor of the hotel, she sees the tower of the cathedral near the *zócalo* and the mountains like a wall

33

behind the city. Thinking that she might be seen from the street, she pulls the curtain halfway over the window.

An old woman dressed in black steps off a bus that has stopped at the corner. A Mustang speeding by honks at a young couple embracing in a doorway across from the hotel. Mara hears a high-pitched voice cursing from somewhere outside.

She puts on a dress and, carrying her sandals, walks barefoot to the door, which she opens without making any noise. In the hallway, she steps into her sandals.

When she reaches the street, she finds that the couple has disappeared. Using the cathedral tower as a guide, she heads toward the *zócalo*. She sees no one, except two young men eating roasted corn on a stoop.

As she nears the square, she hears a brass band playing a fandango, which begins slowly, then speeds up. The band leader lets out a series of yelps that are answered by someone in the crowd. Near Mara, a young boy, maybe fifteen, dances by himself. His legs move like springs, while his hips and shoulders do double time. The people around him whistle. He flashes a smile and spins around, his arms folded behind his back, his white sneakers tapping counterpoint to the rhythm. More whistles. Someone starts clapping and Mara joins in. The boy unfolds his arms, holding them slightly bent at the elbows, his hands open, fingers poised, as if hitting a drumhead.

He beckons to Mara. Everyone seems to be watching them. Cocking his head to one side, the boy waves to her.

Mara makes a few tentative steps and, looking up from the ground, meets the boy's eyes. She begins to dance toward him. The band leader howls like a coyote.

The boy is short—not much taller than Mara herself, so that his head is almost level with hers—his face wide, his skin smooth, reddish-brown. As he dances, his black hair, shaved in back and on the sides but long on top, falls over one eye. Reaching out, he takes her hand and pulls her toward him. With one arm clasping her waist, he holds her close, but not tightly. His slick hair smells of cocoanut, his stiff collar of bleach. As they dance, her fingers slide through his and her arm which is around his neck sticks to his skin. The lights strung between the trees sway in the wind. The clapping grows louder. The faces around them blur into the background. The band pauses, then starts again. The boy draws her closer to him, his stiff jeans rough against her bare legs, his belt buckle pressing into her belly. She opens her hand. He releases it. Putting both arms around his neck, she turns faster, her skirt swishing, the air cooling the backs of her knees, his knee between hers.

After the music has ended, they continue to hold hands.

"*Habla español?*" he asks.

"Yes, but very badly." She laughs, letting go.

He disagrees, then asks her name.

"Mara . . . Marquez."

"Your father is Mexican?"

"No, my husband."

"He's here with you?" He shoots a quick glance behind him.

"At the hotel."

Raising his hand, he makes a rapid gesture, as if to say that then there is nothing to worry about.

She wonders if he is really as young as he looks. "And your name?"

"Hipólito, after my mother's favorite saint." He draws a cross on the ground with the toe of his canvas shoe. "Do you love your husband?"

Surprised, she doesn't answer.

"Why are you here by yourself? Why did you dance with me?" He rubs the cross out with his heel.

"It just happened—I couldn't stop myself." She turns her face away from him. "It's late. I should go back to the hotel."

"Can I walk with you? It's not safe for you to be alone at night."

She shrugs, but accepts.

Rafael is sprawled out in the middle of the bed, his legs and arms flung out, so that his body forms an X. Having set her shoes on a stool to keep the insects from crawling in, Mara pulls off her dress and hangs it over the bedstead. She wonders if she can get into the narrow bed without waking Rafael, lifts the sheet and tries to lie next to him, but there is no space for her. Hoping that he will roll to the other side, she pushes him gently. He wakes.

"Mara?" His voice is thick.

"Rafael, move over and make room for me."

Shifting to the other side, he takes most of the sheet with him. "Did you just get back?"

"Yes." She waits to see whether he is angry.

"Where did you go?"

From his voice, she cannot tell how he feels. "To the *zócalo.*"

"What were you doing there?" He watches her, sucking in his cheeks.

"Dancing."

His face changes, then quickly composes itself. "People don't dance in the *zócalo.*"

"A boy was dancing to a fandango. He was very young, about fifteen. He asked me to dance and I did." She kisses Rafael's fingers.

He shakes his hand free. "And what else?"

"Nothing else."

"Did he kiss you? Did he try to kiss you?"

"No, he was just a kid. He knew I was married." She kicks the twisted sheet away from her ankles.

"How? You don't wear a ring, . . . and you don't look married."

37

"I told him." She laughs. "You don't look married either."

"Why are you looking at me like that?"

Mara and Rafael wait in the car for Remedios.

"I told you everything that happened last night—that nothing happened."

"Did you?" He looks from her mouth to her eyes. "But I think that if he'd tried to fuck you, you would have done it."

"If he had tried, I might have. Because I'm the whore you always paint." She looks out the window.

Remedios raps on the glass. The ends of her reddish hair curl limply, and the outline of her white brassiere shows under her light blouse. She holds tightly onto the strap of the camera that Rafael has given her.

Mara gets out, so that Remedios can climb into the back of the car. With her Nikon dangling from her shoulder, her mother-in-law falls heavily into the Volkswagen.

"I was watching television in the lobby," she explains. "They were interviewing Marta Alvarez, you know, the singer. She just married the painter Chucho González. She said she doesn't like men who put her on a pedestal. When she first met Chucho, he spilled wine on her dress and called her a *puta*. Then she fell in love with him."

Rafael looks sideways at Mara. "Most women are *putas*, especially married women."

38

"Ay, *hijo*. How can you say such things?" Remedios puts on a pair of harlequin sunglasses. "I think Mara looks like Marta," she says to Rafael, as if complimenting him on the resemblance. "Skinny, with long red hair, but Marta's taller and more—" She does not finish the sentence, leaving Mara to wonder what she has that Marta has more of.

The road to Monte Alban is quiet, except for the sound of the car engine and occasional bird cries. Mara rests her chin on her fist and tries to see past the trees and bushes into the adobe houses just beyond. An old man dressed in black and wearing a straw hat, a plaid, mesh market basket in one hand, is walking downhill. He nods to them and tips his hat as they drive past. Rafael returns the nod.

"Marta is Chucho's fourth wife," Remedios says to Rafael.

"Picasso had more women than anyone." He speeds up.

After Rafael parks the car, the three of them start to climb the footpath leading to the plateau. He stays close to his mother, who clutches her camera and complains of the pebbles in her shoes. Walking quickly, Mara reaches the crest of the hill before them. The site below is rectangular, like an air strip, the white pyramids lined up just inside the oblong.

"Ay, *niño,* my feet." Her mother-in-law, supported by Rafael, comes up the path. Mara takes a few steps

39

toward them. Holding the older woman's free arm, she helps her over the last few yards.

"Do you see that arrow-shaped building in the center of the plaza? That's the Observatory—or at least that's what it's called in the guidebook because of the vaulted tunnel that opens on top. Shall we go inside?"

Glancing around as if searching for something, Remedios turns to Rafael. "I would like to sit down."

"The sun is too strong to stay in one place." He frowns at Mara.

The buildings below cast no shadows, although the sun is not yet directly overhead. He points to the opposite side of the plaza where a leafless tree grows next to the base of a small temple. "There? I'll take you down, and you can sit while Mara and I go to the Observatory."

"Ay, no, *hijo*. I'll come with you and then we can rest."

Leading the way, Mara climbs the steps which lead to the front entrance to the Observatory. Below her, Remedios is photographing Rafael, who holds his camera before him, as if he too were taking a picture. Before she enters the building, Mara catches sight of his sheepish, helpless face as he looks away from his mother.

The passageway ahead is lit by sunlight from the doorway from which she has come and another source further along. Following the light, she comes to a

40

THE WHITE MOUNTAIN

second door that opens onto a terrace about a hundred feet above the ground. The masonry is decorated with large bas-reliefs of plumed men. She hears voices.

And Luz? ... *What happened to her daughter? The tall one?*

Didn't you hear? ... *last summer, only sixteen years old* ...

She didn't wear a white dress?

The whole family talked about it. .... *Someone saw her alone with him* ... *She had a good excuse, of course.*

She left—just like that?

She said she needed some air, and when she came back ... *told some story* ...

The voices are very loud.

Both Rafael and Remedios appear surprised to see Mara on the terrace.

"All those steps." Remedios leans against one of the plumed men.

Rafael aims his camera at the other end of the wall, then places it in a niche in the rocks, sets the timer, and strikes a pose. The shutter clicks.

They arrive in Tehuantepec at about four o'clock in the afternoon, and find a hotel close to the road, a large white stucco building with a sign advertising an *alberca*—a swimming pool, Rafael explains. He stops the car before the office and, rolling down the window, leans out.

A stocky Indian woman in a print housedress

41

comes out. "A room? We have many rooms. Four hundred pesos a night. Two beds."

Rafael looks at Mara.

"About thirty dollars? I guess that's O.K." She nudges him with her elbow, whispering in English. "One room?"

Remedios makes a face. "It's not modern, but they do have a pool."

Rafael glances at her in the rear view mirror. "I'm tired of driving. Let's stop here for a night. If you don't like it, we can change tomorrow." He pays the woman, and she gives him a key.

"The third room on the right side of the patio. You can take the car to the other side."

Mara unlocks the door. The room is middle-sized and rectangular, the headboards of the twin beds against a long, pistachio-colored wall. A wooden wardrobe stands in one corner. The windows face the street. She pulls up the shade. The sky is purplish, and a man is leading an ox by a rope. Playing with the threads of the lemon-yellow spread, she sits on the edge of one of the beds.

Remedios appears in the doorway. "It's almost night." She sighs, then comes in and sits down next to Mara. "What is the English word for this part of the day?"

"Twilight . . . or dusk."

42

"I'm always sad at this time." Her mouth slackens. "Rafael is angry with me, no?"

"I don't think so. Why should he be?"

Her mother-in-law's eyelids look puffy, but maybe no more than usual. "His voice is so angry when he speaks to me."

"He's tired, that's all. Don't worry. If he's angry, it's probably something I did, not you." She pats the older woman's hand, but somehow her own gesture embarrasses her. Turning to avoid Remedios' eyes, she notices a colored postcard of the Virgin of Guadalupe taped to the night table.

Her mother-in-law sees the image too, and it seems to reassure her. *"La Santa María* is everywhere. When Rafael had bronchitis and the doctors gave him an injection of penicillin, he had an allergic reaction that almost killed him. I prayed to Her on my knees for hours not to take him from me. *La Virgen* always listens."

Mara stares at the gold and white flecks in the pink linoleum floor, then at the aureole around the Virgin. She wishes that Remedios would stop talking. Putting her hand on the other woman's shoulder, she waits, then says, "It's so hot in here. I'm going to sit outside." As she pushes open the screen door, she turns. "Shall I leave it open?"

Remedios shakes her head. "No, the mosquitos will come in."

43

From a chair on the tiled veranda bordering the patio, Mara watches a bluish, unsteady light coming from the office. She gets up and crosses the scrubby lawn, walking halfway around a large, kidney-shaped pool sunk into the center of the court.

A young girl stands by the cash register, resting her face and hands on the counter, not watching the soundless television picture behind her.

"It's very quiet here," Mara ventures.

"It's late in the season. Everyone went last week." Speaking without expression, she raises her head. "The Mexicans come in December, the Americans in January, February, and May, and the French in July and August. The French left last week."

"Who stays?"

The girl places her hand on her chest. "We live here all year round. Sometimes people come at strange times, like you. There's no one else here tonight."

"The rest of the hotel is empty?"

"Yes. We didn't expect anyone. That's why we drained the swimming pool this morning."

The girl stares at the flies crawling across the counter. Her voice is high-pitched and tentative, her hair plaited in two braids. She could be a child or a woman. Behind her, the television screen alternates between close-ups of a tense, pale face and a shiny black one.

44

"Mission Impossible?"

The girl looks at her blankly, then at the program and shakes her head. A fly lands on her shoulder, where it remains for a few seconds, its forelegs clasped together.

The door opens. Rafael's hair is wet. He has shaved and changed his clothes. "I was looking for you. Remedios said you were sitting in the patio."

She smiles. "I wanted to see what was on television."

Outside, she touches his cheek. "Your face is smooth."

"Are you having a good time?"

She doesn't answer immediately. "Going to Monte Alban was like walking up a hill and finding a mysterious, but familiar dream."

"And Remedios?"

"I would rather be alone with you."

"I wanted to take her somewhere, to do something for her. For you too," he adds. "For both of you."

"But she wanted to go to Acapulco and stay in a big hotel and eat dinner in a fancy restaurant every night."

"She said she wanted to see the ruins with us."

"She wants to sit in the ruins."

"Is there water in the pool?"

"Some, not enough to swim."

She walks around to the shallow end and sits on

45

the rim, so that her feet dangle over the water. He follows.

"Instead of in the room with your mother, let's sleep outside tonight."

"It will get cold later on."

Although he sounds serious, when she looks up, he smiles at her. She reaches out and tugs at the bottoms of his jeans. "Take off your shoes."

Kneeling beside her, he strokes her hair. "And your dress? Will you take it off?"

"If I do, what will happen?" She leans her head against his knees. He pushes her hair aside and kisses her ear. A mosquito buzzes close to them. She waves it away. Pointing her toe, she draws a circle on the floor of the pool, raising up a flurry of insects.

She lowers herself into the water, which rises over her ankles. Splashing her dress as she goes, she wades to the center. The tiles are scummy, and she steps carefully, so as not to slip. Although the sky is still red along the horizon, the moon and a few stars are already out. The air is hot and damp, dense with clouds of gnats. Mara rolls her dress to her waist; then, leaning over, she wets her wrists and the insides of her elbows. She walks slowly forward to where the water is clearer and cooler and comes almost to her knees. Bending down, she dunks her head. The chlorine stings her eyes and she comes up quickly.

Rafael stands on the other end—a long, narrow

silhouette with broad, slightly hunched shoulders, the right one higher than the left.

She puts her face in the water again, trying to hold her breath and stay under longer than before. Someone splashes her (it must be Rafael). She opens her eyes. Blurred by darkness, he is close to her. Only his teeth show clearly.

"Where do you begin?" She reaches out her hand to touch him, but does not. She moves her hand to the left, still nothing; to the right, she feels skin.

From the direction of the office, she hears a door slam. For a moment the patio is lit blue; the water glistens. A pair of pants and a white shirt float on the surface.

THE OPENING

Through the holes in the window shade, late afternoon sunlight scatters over the objects in the room—an empty bookshelf, the suitcase, Rafael's portfolio, a transistor radio—all rectangular, sharp lines—the plaid blanket over the bed another rectangle. Mexico is tiring her—living with Remedios, keeping out of her way; the cafés and parties and dinner parties where people talk too quickly for her to understand completely, the afternoon rains, the heat. In the mornings, she stays in bed as long as possible, shops at the *mercado* with Rafael, is glad to come back for the siesta, when they lie together in this small room, talking, sleeping.

A mosquito settles on the wall. Her sandal is on the floor. Raising it slowly, she aims, but the insect flits away toward the ceiling. She stands on the bed and smashes it, leaving a small, dark stain on the wall.

She hears footsteps coming up the stairs and gets down from the bed to open the door. Rafael holds a tray with two cups of coffee and a can of condensed milk, which he places beside the bed. One cup slides, spilling coffee onto the saucer.

"Clumsy." She touches his wrist, then reaches across him for a cup.

Leaning against the pillow, she tastes the coffee, adds more milk, stirs. "You remembered spoons today." She watches him: hair, eyebrows, eyes, nose, ears, mouth, teeth (he smiles), eyes again. She sets down her cup.

"The invitation says the opening begins at seven." He waves his hand impatiently. "We should be there on time." His head turned away from her, he seems to be staring at his portfolio.

She puts her cheek to his, scratching her face on the shaved skin.

He hangs his arm around her neck, lets it dangle there for a minute, takes it away.

"Does that mean I should get dressed?" The tiles are cold under her bare feet.

"I don't want to be late—not to my own show." He finishes his coffee, continues to talk. "Many people will be there because they are curious what hap-

49

pens to a painter and his work after living in New York . . ."

She stops listening and, playfully, sticks out her tongue, his gesture.

He bends down, kisses her thigh. "I told Ascencio we'd pick him up."

"Does he still dislike me?" Opening the suitcase, she unfolds a cotton sun dress.

"He thought you were a woman who tries to control men. I told him he was wrong—you're not like that. He can see you better now. It's not you. He's afraid of all women." Rafael is on his side, head resting on his knuckles. "I like that dress."

"Why?" She loops the straps, ties a bow at the shoulder.

"It shows your legs, your back, a lot of skin." He makes a quick move, as if to grab her.

She dodges his hand. "Do you think it will upset your mother?"

"She said she's not coming. She says my drawings are pornographic. Already, she's scandalized—by me, by my work." He shrugs. "She thinks we're both crazy. Me—because I'm a painter; you—because you're with me."

"Is she right?" Mara smiles.

The front door opens and closes. She isn't sure if Remedios has come in or gone out. The sound of running water, cabinets slammed, pots rattling. She thinks that she hears the blender humming. A few

50

minutes later, a high-heeled step comes up the stairs, crosses the landing to the bedroom next to theirs.

Mara raises the window shade. Outside, the sun, low above the city, streaks the sky violet. In the courtyard of the warehouse next door, the workers are joking, their voices and laughter loud, somehow disturbing. A man in a straw hat, sweeping the patio, looks up. She pulls down the shade.

Rafael tugs at her strap. She pushes his hand aside. He undoes the bow; the bodice sags. He bites her, a little roughly.

"You always taste like cocoanut." He zips his jacket.

She reties the strings in a double knot.

They wait in front of the heavy wooden door of Ascencio's parents' house. The street, just off El Parque de la Revolucíon, is quiet. The low building is stuccoed and painted a mustard color, its tall windows covered by metal grates, the shutters closed, as if no one were home.

She hears whispering, someone walking carefully, then Ascencio's voice. A shutter opens. His face appears.

"I was waiting for you in the patio. I wasn't sure if I heard the bell. You only rang once?"

Mara and Rafael follow Ascencio through a series of small, dark rooms, the last one crowded with wardrobes, lamps, stacks of books, an upholstered armchair. In a wall niche, a candle burns before a saint's image, her face chipped away.

They step out onto the veranda.

"My father's *orquídeas*." Ascencio motions toward the jumble of potted plants which rings the patio.

In the courtyard, a great many drawings are arranged close together, like pieces of mosaic.

"I brought more than a hundred drawings with me." Ascencio waves his hands in the air.

Squatting on his heels, Indian-style, Rafael looks at the work, spread out so that it almost completely covers the tiled floor of the enclosure. His face is expressionless. "These drawings are different here in Mexico. They seemed stranger in New York."

Mara knows that he does not like his friend's work, wonders if Ascencio knows.

"They belong here." Ascencio folds his arms across his chest.

He has used heavy black ink on white, thick-grained paper, eighteen by twenty-four inch sheets, bold lines curving into monstrous human figures in grotesque postures. All have Ascencio's long nose, the male figures his forked beard.

"All together—they're wonderful . . . The lines are strong, and the effect of so many drawings together . . ." She does not finish.

"I think of them as one piece, the panels of a mural—a monument." He lifts his arm high above his head, as if indicating its height.

Rafael stands in the shade of an avocado tree. He and Mara exchange glances.

"Like all the frames of a film stretched out before you . . ." Again, she trails off.

Rafael strips a leaf from the tree, rolls it into a tube, chews the end. "What are you going to do with this mural?" One hand shadows his face; the other is in his pocket.

"I'd like to show it here, but I don't want it next to anything else. It needs a whole wall—a great room, big enough so that people can stand away and see it all at once. I need a huge space—a museum."

The orchids are different from those she has seen in the States. They grow from cones like dry cornhusks. Ranging from brick to mustard (none of the delicate pinks, violets, or pale yellows of a florist's corsage), some spotted, some streaked, one petal lolling—a fleshy tongue—the flowers gape, open-mouthed, more animals than plants.

"Orchids don't bite, although some have teeth. They're parasites, cling to other plants like bats on a branch." Ascencio points to an upper limb of the avocado tree from which hangs a brownish sac resembling a bird's nest.

Nodding at a drawing of a human-headed creature performing auto-fellatio, Rafael grins. "If you showed these pieces here, they would really shock people."

"They frighten people in New York. Imagine how the Mexican bourgeoisie would react."

"My mother thinks my drawings are obscene—although she can't figure out what's going on in them—she thinks something is going on. She doesn't want to come to my opening tonight because she is afraid of what people will say to her."

"Everyone here thinks in the same way." Ascencio frowns.

Half-listening, she examines a greenish-brown orchid, darker spots in a circular pattern on its petals, which give off a strong smell of chocolate. "May I pick this one?" she asks.

The two men face each other across the drawings: Rafael, back toward her, black jeans and shirt, black hair; Ascencio, looking in her direction, in a white jump suit, legs straddled, arms folded over his chest. The sun goes behind a cloud, leaving the sky a pale gray wash. Water spatters the tiled courtyard. The men do not move.

"The drawings," she calls out, running into the rain.

Both men drop to their knees.

Ascencio opens the Volkswagen door for her and waits.

"I'll sit up front with Rafael." Pushing the seat down, she motions for him to get in.

They drive along Chapultepec, past the fountains, swelled from the rain, which divide the wide street down the center. They turn right at La Paz.

"There's La Chava's house." Rafael points out a white stuccoed mansion on the corner, its garden dense with bushes and tall palms, a veranda along the wall, purple bougainvilleas climbing over the balcony.

"One of your old lovers?" she teases.

He turns off the windshield wipers. "She's a very rich woman who collects art. Before I came to New York, she bought two of my drawings at an auction."

"How much did she pay?" Ascencio taps the back of Mara's seat.

"Not much. Four hundred pesos for one, six hundred and fifty for the other; but that was two years ago, and they were small drawings too." He rubs the back of his neck. "Now my prices have gone up."

"La Chava? Is she beautiful?" Mara presses her palms together.

"She's not young—maybe more than fifty—she has a daughter older than you. But she likes painters. I have a friend—Mara, you know Felix—who painted big, red hearts with arrows and 'Felix loves La Chava' on the sidewalk in front of her house. It's still there."

"He loves her because she buys his work." Ascencio continues to drum on Mara's seat.

"Her husband—he's super straight, an engineer— he was very angry." Rafael laughs.

"Is her daughter beautiful?" She keeps her hands in her lap.

"When a woman is rich, she doesn't need to be beautiful," says Ascencio. The sound of his restless fingers stops.

Her hair catches on something. "What does a woman need?" She jerks her head, freeing her hair.

"To stay rich." Ascencio lets out a couple of yelps. Rafael laughs again.

Stooping because of the low doorway, she steps into the first gallery. Rafael and Ascencio follow.

The exconvento is a sixteenth-century building, a converted cloister, with a high, vaulted ceiling. The masonry is pale, sandy—limestone, Rafael tells Mara.

As they enter, a tall man in a blue sports shirt, accompanied by a blond woman, greets them.

"Rafael." They shake hands and embrace.

"De Soto, . . . this is Mara."

The woman is thin and wears a black dress. She touches De Soto's arm. He extends his hand, but seems to be waiting for something.

"My wife." Rafael speaks hesitantly, as if this does not properly explain their connection. "And Ascencio, who also lives in New York—although he is from Mexico."

"I am a painter, an actor, a botanist, a magician." Ascencio curls one end of his mustache around his finger.

A waiter with a tray of glasses offers them red wine.

"They serve cognac for the big openings." Ascencio winks at De Soto.

Looking pained, the director says jovially, "I think

56

you are mistaken, my friend. We never serve cognac. Even when we had a show of Tapies, we served wine. French wine, of course." He raises his glass.

The woman, introduced as Gabrielle, leans toward Rafael and, speaking Spanish with a French accent, asks him how he likes the way his exhibition is hung.

He pushes his hair from his forehead. "The guy who did it is very good. He understands exactly how work needs to be put on the walls. He looks around the space, tells his assistant to spread out the pieces and lean them against the walls. Then he stands there for a few minutes, quiet, thinking. All of a sudden, he starts pointing, saying 'There, there, to the left, no— higher,' and in an hour the show is up, everything perfect."

Mara listens to the talk, the Spanish becoming hard for her to follow, especially the French woman's. Not speaking, she stares at Gabrielle's tanned wrist, small gold watch, red fingernails. Rafael appears to be listening to something that she is saying.

Mara stands on her toes and whispers in his ear, "I'm afraid I've drunk too much." Her lips almost touch him. The French woman continues to talk.

Glass in hand, Rafael puts his arm around Mara, spilling wine on her dress.

"Ay, *cabrón*." Ascencio slaps his knee.

"*Pobrecita.*" Gabrielle takes a handkerchief, tucked between her breasts, and starts wiping Mara off. "You need to use cold water, or it will stain."

"The bathroom?"

"It's upstairs. I'll show you." She links arms with Mara.

They stand before the mirror, their eyes meeting in the reflection. She wonders how old Gabrielle is. Mara's cheeks flush, while the rest of her face remains pale.

The other woman wets a wad of paper towels. "Rafael, he is your husband?"

"Yes."

"How long?" Lifting Mara's skirt, she begins to rub the spot.

"A month. We got married because of his mother. She wouldn't have let us stay in her house otherwise."

"But you live together in New York?"

"For two years."

Gabrielle's hand shows under the wet cloth. "It's almost out. Can you see anything?"

"It's still a little pink."

"He's very handsome, no?" She turns on the faucet, holds another towel under the water.

"Rafael? People say that—I didn't think so when I first met him. I thought he was a little ugly." She giggles.

"Women like ugly men." Gabrielle brushes the wet spot with her hand. "There, it's out."

Smoothing her damp skirt over her legs, Mara

glances again in the mirror, avoiding the other woman's eyes.

Gabrielle takes a lipstick from her evening bag, colors her lower lip, presses both lips together, smiles.

When they return, Rafael is in the same corner where they left him, along with Ascencio, De Soto, and others whom Mara does not know.

"Women always come back from the bathroom looking as if they have told each other all their secrets." De Soto's eyes are on Gabrielle.

"They look like they've armed themselves to the teeth and are ready to take on any man." Ascencio straightens his shoulders.

The French woman says to Rafael, "The show is beautiful. I don't like most art I see, but these prints are wonderful."

De Soto immediately agrees. "Ricardo Cervantes Morales, the critic for *El Informador,* is here. He's not saying anything—that's a good sign. If he were going to pan it, he'd be admiring everything."

"Critics don't know anything. They don't paint, so they don't really understand painting. The only ones who can criticize art are the artists themselves." Rafael's laugh comes from his throat; his teeth show, but no sound. The whites of his eyes are dirty, as if the color from the iris has bled. He holds his glass loosely, seeming ready to let go completely, then sways to one

59

side, bumping into Gabrielle. Her faint smile remains fixed.

On the opposite wall hang a pair of portraits, which Mara recognizes. She takes a step toward them.

"Where are you going?" Ascencio says abruptly, stopping her.

"To look at the prints."

"Haven't you seen them all before?" Gabrielle sucks in her cheeks.

"Of course, but it's different to see them framed and in a gallery." Mara notices a smudge on her ankle, which she tries to rub off with her heel.

"Nobody comes to an opening to see the work." Ascencio claps his hands. "But let's go. I want to see Rafael's drawings too."

Everyone laughs.

The spotlights reflect on the glass over the portraits of a woman and a bestial male figure. The woman is copied from a photograph that Rafael took of her. On that day, her hair was loosely twisted into a bun, but in the print the arrangement is abstracted into a mass of angles. The woman faces forward, her eyes meeting the viewer's, while her body leans toward the print's edge, her right arm lifted in the direction of the other portrait.

"You and Rafael?" Ascencio speaks quietly.

"He did it last year. In May. You never saw it before?"

"No."

"Were you in New York then?" She can't remember.

"I was in Mexico for six months last year."

"I think we saw you when you got back. You showed us photographs you had taken of your father's orchids."

"I went many times with my father into the jungle to hunt *orquídeas.*"

"Did you find any?"

"My father discovered a new species, which he calls *pardalinata* because of its leopard spots." He seeems to focus on some part of her neck.

She tests her strap. "The greenish one I saw in your patio?"

"That one. It's very complicated because he and another orchid specialist came upon it at the same time." Eyebrows raised, he pauses, as if for greater effect. "My father claims it as his discovery and so does the other guy."

"How did that happen?"

His voice grows excited again. "A botanist from Veracruz, Enrique Goetz Guzman, invited my father and me to go with him to hunt for orchids in the Sierra de Talpa in Jalisco. After a series of accidents, which forced us to sleep one night with only the sky for covering and left us with very little drinking water and no food at all, we started back through a pine-oak forest unknown to my father."

61

"How many days without food?"

"Two days. No—longer. Two and a half days." He pulls in his stomach.

Her strap has slipped off her shoulder. She pushes it up.

Carrying a glass of wine in each hand, Rafael comes toward them. He gives one to Mara.

"*Cabrón.* None for me?" Ascencio holds out his empty palms.

"You've got to get your own, *compadre.* This is mine." He hooks his arm around her neck and, throwing his head back, finishes his wine in one swallow.

She offers her glass to Ascencio. "What happened in the forest?"

"Come on, *compadre,* what happened in the forest?" Rafael's silent laughter.

Ascencio drinks the wine, returns the empty glass. "I was walking behind my father and Goetz, looking up at the trees, when I heard them both cry out. They had caught sight of a large mass of orchid cones which had started to develop flower spikes. They both collected samples and cultivated the plants. When my father's specimen bloomed, he decided it was a new species and wrote a monograph announcing his discovery. Goetz did the same thing, only he gave it his own name."

"Who has the rightful claim to the orchid?" She rubs the rim of her glass against her lower lip. "They both came upon it at the same time."

62

He fiddles with the crystal skull around his neck.
She touches the faint pink spot on her dress.

Ascencio glances at Rafael, who seems not to be
listening.

She and Rafael sit in the car in Remedios' driveway.
"Mara?"

She turns to him.

He averts his head, so that she can only see his
profile, then he faces her.

"I know." She opens the glove compartment, then
slams it closed. "Please don't say anything." She feels
his stare, as she watches the black cloth of his shirt rise
and fall.

"You think you know." The headlights of an ap-
proaching car strike his face. He shuts his eyes. The car
passes.

"I didn't understand what he meant."

"He's not interested in you. He wants to hurt me."

"He's your friend."

"Let's go upstairs." He makes a gesture, as if to spin
the steering wheel. It doesn't move.

"What are we going to do?"

"Fuck."

"I'm tired."

"You're always tired." His fingers clench the wheel.

She keeps her voice low. "Your mother makes me
tired, so do your friends, dealers, collectors, prices,
Picasso, Chucho Gonzales. It all makes me tired."

63

For a few minutes, they say nothing.

She unrolls the window. "Can you smell the honeysuckle? It's so sweet this evening."

"*La madreselva* smells very strong at night. It can make you drunk if you get too close."

"Who told you that?"

"My grandmother."

THE PERFORMANCE

She sits on a black cushion, her shoes on the floor beside her. Since she returned to New York two weeks ago, she is getting used to being without Rafael. She rarely thinks of him until someone asks her when he is coming back, and she realizes, as she tries to answer, that she does not know.

Three days after she had left Mexico, he called to tell her that Remedios needed an operation. He was vague, mentioned a female problem, a hysterectomy maybe. His mother wanted him to stay with her for a while. He might have to be in Guadalajara a month or more.

65

"I can't stand being away from you. Away from my paintings, away from New York."

"It's hard for me too," she said, although it was really not so difficult.

A slight, Japanese man carrying a small black case walks to the left side of the space, near Mara. His hair is short and bristly. He takes off his jeans and sweater; underneath he wears tights and a shirt, both purple. Facing the audience, he sits, crosses his legs, his case before him. As he peers into a mirror set into the lid, he ties a cloth around his head. He unscrews a jar, scoops out some greasepaint, rubbing it between his palms, then deftly whitens his face and neck. Putting his finger into another tin, he then applies red to his eyelids, cheeks, mouth. After a quick, careful look at his reflection, he stands up and, taking a sword from the case, straps it to his waist. Taped music begins to play.

At the sound of wood blocks clapped together, the man, his sheathed sword in both hands, glares at the audience and starts to circle the floor. Snarling, with stylized steps, he advances, his toes splayed. Drums beat—the music quickens. His red-rimmed eyes cross with the appearance of intense emotion. He lurches with angular movements, turning his head from side to side. With legs spread and knees bent, he draws the sword and, brandishing it, spans the floor in a series of jumps, his body rigid, his expression fierce. Suddenly, he seems to lose control. His arms and legs flail, his eyes roll. He groans. Dropping his sword, he staggers from one end of the space to the other, pulling his hair like a madman. The music ends abruptly. He stands motionless, then bows.

The dancer goes again to his case. He puts on a red, flowered kimono over his clothes, binds a gold obi around his torso, sets a geisha wig on his head. Holding a one-stringed samisen, he flops down with mock dignity and coyly eyes the audience. The taped voice of a woman sings slowly, accompanied by a samisen. As he mimes playing the instrument, he jerks his head, mouthing the words and making absurd coquettish faces. Rolling his eyes so that only the whites show, he moves with greater abandon, screeches, drowning out the singer. Still seated, he sways, rocking back and forth. Then, giving up all pretense of plucking the single string, he rips it from the samisen, which he smashes against the floor. With increasing frenzy, he continues until the singing ends. For a few seconds, he lies still, apparently exhausted, his wig askew, the instrument's broken neck in his left hand.

Again, Mara thinks of Rafael, oddly, now her husband. He said that they were married before they were married, but she has never felt this way. After the ceremony, Rafael hardly spoke. That evening he passed out on the sofa. His head lay in her lap when he turned to one side and, without opening his eyes, vomited on the red corduroy upholstery.

67

She reads the program. In the last piece, Soseki will play a Buddhist priest. A low chant drones over the tape. He takes off the kimono, then the tights and shirt, leaving only a white cloth, passed between his legs and wound around his waist, his smooth body uncovered. Bells and gongs embellish the voices. Carrying a scroll painted with large black characters, he unfurls the paper like a herald as he presents it to different sections of the audience. His arms spread out at his sides, as if to maintain balance, he walks slowly, dipping at intervals.

He sets down the scroll, then begins to dance with quick, light steps, but carelessly, throwing himself this way and that. He dances faster, stepping on the people sitting closest to him, stumbling and almost falling on them. A woman cries angrily, "Hey, watch it!" but he takes no notice and keeps spinning.

As he approaches Mara, he reaches out his hand to her and, as he passes, lifts her from the floor. She slides after him in her stocking feet, hopping and turning, trying to follow. They circle the space once. Then, as they pass her cushion again, he lets her go. She is flushed, breathless. He is reeling. The clanging percussion intensifies. He stops in the center of the floor and undoes his loincloth, which falls into white folds around his feet. He bows deeply to loud applause.

Mara stands on one foot as she puts the other into her shoe. Soseki, in a man's cotton kimono, comes up to her.

68

"Thank you for dancing with me." He is out of breath and pants between words.

She smiles at him.

He lowers his voice. "I would like to see you again." His face is smooth and round, as if there were no skull under the skin. Through the streaked make-up, she can make out his features—a fine nose, bowed lips. He blinks rapidly several times.

"Yes." She cannot distinguish the pupil in the black iris. Taking a pen from her pocket, she writes her name and telephone number in the corner of the program, then hands it to him.

"Mara," he reads aloud. "It sounds Japanese."

"So does Soseki." They both laugh.

Soseki, in a black tee-shirt and jeans, gets up from the floor and, without speaking, begins to walk, the same dipping step that he used in the performance. He beckons. The dancers follow in single file, snaking around the room, each one doing a version of Soseki's walk.

Mara watches his feet, counting so as not to lose the rhythm. Keeping her shoulders relaxed but not slumped, she holds her head up, her back straight.

Soseki's legs move with his arms—as the right leg steps forward, the right arm flies up too. He looks like Barrault walking in place before a moving backdrop in *Les Enfants du Paradis*. Dripping with sweat, his face dark from exertion, he stops. With his hands

69

clasped together, he thanks the dancers and dismisses them.

She feels her own skin, which is dry. A blond woman continues to practice, examining herself in the large mirrors, her face distorted from the effort. Mara wants to smooth the woman's forehead with her hand.

Blinking as he looks about, Soseki, in an old tweed overcoat, a plaid wool scarf hanging loose, enters the dressing room. He lights a cigarette, purses his woman's lips around it. "I'm glad you came. How was the class?"

"I couldn't concentrate."

"I knew you were thinking about other things. You could be a dancer, but your mind is too full. You have a dancer's body, though, strong legs, a strong back."

"When I was a little girl, I wanted to dance, but I was totally undisciplined. I didn't want to work at anything."

"What did you do?" He throws the butt on the floor, steps on it with the heel of his shoe.

"I stayed in bed reading books. Sometimes, I went into the living room and read on the sofa. That's how I learned about the world. That's why I'm never quite sure what's real and what's not."

They go to a Japanese restaurant where they both order sushi. Mara has soup first.

Although she is used to chopsticks, she has difficulty getting the small, slippery mushrooms at the bottom of the bowl. She picks one out with her fingers.

Soseki looks surprised. "You're very charming, like a child, when you do that, but . . ."

"But I am a child, Soseki. Haven't you noticed? If it bothers you, then I won't do it." She lifts her spoon.

He calls the waiter over. "Whiskey for me, on the rocks. Saki for my friend." He squints at her through cigarette smoke. "Some dancers I know are doing a piece on the Lower East Side. I think it will be good. Do you want to come?"

They turn north at Second Avenue. She pulls her beret over her ears and puts her hands in her pockets. Soseki, hatless, gloveless, smoking jauntily, walks next to her.

The space on East Eleventh Street is oval-shaped. Red-carpeted stepped rows rise up along its sides like an amphitheater.

Soseki introduces Mara to a Japanese couple, both painters. The man asks if she is a dancer.

"No."

"Well, what are you then?" The woman stares at her.

"I don't know." Mara assumes a blank expression. She does not want to explain herself.

Soseki smiles at her.

71

A few minutes later, when they have taken their seats, he leans toward her. "I really liked what you said."

"What did I say?"

He whispers in her ear, his lips brushing her skin. "That you don't know what you are, who you are. I love uncertainty."

In the center of the oval, a black banner hides the bodies of actors, only their white tabi showing, like feet of a giant centipede. To a rushing sound like wind or sea, the flag unfurls, and six performers step out, led by a woman in a red skirt, bare-shouldered, a purple bandeau over her breasts. Her head is wrapped in white cloth, to which is bound a crab that waves its front claws helplessly, opening and closing its pincers as it reaches upward. Another woman, dressed in red, an open fan behind her head like a halo, stands at the end of the line. She carries a paper fish, which she places on the floor. The four men in loincloths, their bodies painted white, crouch before the flag. They too wear crabs and slowly crawl about the oval. Grimacing, one of the men rises. The woman with the fan, simpering foolishly, scuttles away from him.

Soseki touches Mara's hand. "Let's go. I don't want to watch others now."

He opens the door to his apartment and remains in the hallway for a minute to slip off his shoes, which he places inside by the entrance. She takes off her

72

boots and puts them next to the shoes. He drapes his coat over the back of a chair. She hesitates, then unfastens hers and lays it over his, stuffing her beret into the pocket.

"Would you like some tea?"

"Can I help you make it?" she offers.

"You are my guest. Please sit down."

She kneels on a mat near the radiator, while he sets the kettle on the fire, then carefully measures tea leaves into a pot. When the water boils, he pours some into the teapot and some into the cups to warm them. Bringing the tea things on a tray, he places them before Mara and, facing her, sits down, tucking his legs underneath him.

Looking at each other, they wait in silence for the tea to brew. He checks his watch.

"Ah, it's ready now."

She smiles. "You time your tea?"

"It must be just right, not too strong, not weak either. I can tell by the color, but with a clock it's more accurate."

She runs her finger around the outer rim of her cup.

"In Japan, only demons have red hair, long red hair." He grins.

"I'm not a demon." Mara unclips her hair, letting it fall loose.

"It's lovely, like red silk." He reaches forward and gently draws his fingers through it.

As his hand passes her cheek, she turns her head

and bites his wrist with equal delicacy, ending with her tongue, not teeth, on his skin.

The radiator clatters like two objects hit together.

They move closer to each other. He pushes aside her hair, slowly kisses the nape of her neck. Bending her head, she holds her body very still. His throat is smooth as teak. She twists around and rubs her face in his spiked hair. Leaning back slightly, she slips one hand under his sweater, running it down the side of his body and across his belly. As she takes his chin in her other hand, she nibbles his lower lip with small, precise bites, from corner to corner. His mouth tastes of cigarettes, his hair of something that she does not recognize.

They back away from each other. Straightening up, he rolls his head, as if trying to work out a cramp, then snaps it back. His eyes widen briefly, in pain or surprise.

He pulls off his pullover. Underneath, his chest is bare, his nipples dark, small. She looks down at her own sweater. Using both hands, he unbuttons her cardigan. As he pushes the sweater off her shoulders, pulling the sleeves over her wrists, she catches hold of it, reluctant to let him draw it away. For a moment, they have the sweater between them.

The radiator bangs loudly, as if someone has struck it with a hammer. Mara lets go; the sweater falls on the mat. She approaches him on her knees.

Clasping her legs around his waist, without touch-

74

ing him with her hands, she presses her body to his, her breasts flattened against his chest. She reaches under his armpits, smoothing his back with her palms, fingers tensed, open, and, crossing her ankles, locks her feet behind him. He freezes, jerks his head back, his eyes at once wild and serene.

An envelope with the familiar red and green striped border has been slipped under the door. She picks it up, recognizes Rafael's handwriting. The postmark is a week old. Hooking her finger in the loose flap in the corner, she tears the envelope open.

Dear Mara,
I'm sorry if I sound upset or depressed. It seems to me like a dream or an acid trip. It's very strange not to be with you. My mother is feeling better, but she still says she needs me. She always sends her love to you. I feel very bad. No, I don't even know what I feel. I can't draw. I can't paint. I'm not able to do anything. I feel crazy. I think I'm not adapted—I wasn't before, but now it's worse. I feel like I will never go back to New York. I'm wondering what is going on with you.

He thinks I have a lover, she says aloud to herself.

This city is making me crazy. I want to work but here I can't concentrate. My mind is just flying. I have no ideas. You are 2,000 miles away, my paintings too—everything I

75

really want is far from me, but also very close, only five hours by plane. I hope these things pass soon. Your lover that loves you.

Rafael Marquez, October 19, 1976.

He has signed and dated the letter as if it were a painting.

She puts the letter back into the envelope, then walks over to the chest, lifts its cover and, feeling under the clothes on top, sticks the envelope between the folded sheets.

She unlocks the door and waits while Soseki goes in first. From across the street, the lights of the building stare in like searchlights. The loft is very cold. She stands on the desk and turns on the space heater.

"You live surrounded by demons." He gestures toward the paintings.

"These are Rafael's—his monstrous children." She keeps her coat on, but takes off her gloves and lays them on the table.

Stretched out on the couch, she watches him walk from painting to painting. She wonders if he finds Rafael's work crude.

He stops in front of the unfinished canvas on the easel, begun before they had gone to Mexico. A woman—actually, only a head and trunk—a red tongue darting from her mouth like a flame—faces a gigantic skull. Flowers and little skulls are sketched in the background.

"One of my aspects." She leans back on her elbows, her feet on the arm of the sofa.

"You could be a terrible woman." Sitting down beside her, he lights a cigarette, dropping the match into a clear glass ashtray. "It's very cold in here." He takes her hands, which she is warming between her thighs, and presses them between his own.

"I told you it would be cold." The match flickers, goes out, still glowing.

"You know Bob is sleeping in the apartment tonight. I think he had a fight with his lover." Bending over her, Soseki pushes her hair from her face. "Let's go to a hotel. It will be warm, the bed will be made, there will be two pillows, a bathtub, soap in little bars, a color television set; and when we leave in the morning, we can take the towels." He smiles.

"It's hard to explain why, but I can't go." Impossible. It was too adult—adulterous, in fact.

He speaks quietly, without annoyance. "I think I understand you."

She sits up, drawing her knees up to her chest, grasps her ankles. "Soseki, Rafael called me one morning after I'd spent the night at your apartment. He told me he'd tried to phone me the night before, very late, two or three o'clock, and I wasn't home. He asked me where I'd been. I said with friends. He asked me if I had another lover. I said no. I lied to him. I've never lied to him before. I wanted to tell him, but I couldn't. I was afraid that he'd never come back, that I'd never see him again." She puts her hand over her mouth, biting her knuckles to keep from crying.

Soseki strokes her hair. "I know it's very hard for you. You're very young. You've never had a lover. You believed in your own loyalty. Now you're unsure. You don't understand why you need a lover. You think you have done something wrong. I'm sorry you feel that way."

"Maybe later, I will tell him." Mara looks at the large painting hanging above the couch. She stares into the eyes of the man without arms, one of Rafael's self-portraits. She tries to remember his face—eyebrows, eyes, nose, lips, teeth, cheeks, chin—but she cannot reconstruct it. Touching the canvas, she wishes that he were back.

THE RETURN

As Mara passes through one of the Greek sculpture halls, she notices a young man, a camera around his neck, leaning against the base of a statue of a young boy. Lithe, with short, curly hair, he resembles a satyr. He catches her eye, and she quickly turns away to study a wounded Amazon, a gash in her marble breast. Hoping that the man will not come after her, she walks slowly into the next gallery.

In the room's center, light slanting in from the high windows, surrounded by potted plants, a monumental Aphrodite stands on an elevated platform, her arms broken off at the shoulders, her plump belly

shadowing her navel. Mara hears a click behind her
and glances around. His back toward her, facing a
frieze of a battle scene, the man with the camera
stands a few feet away. He is motionless, his hands in
his pockets. She does not see him again that afternoon; except, as she is leaving, she thinks that she
sees him peek out from behind a sarcophagus.

"I thought he was following me."

"If I saw you in a museum, I would follow you
too." Soseki reaches over the side of the bed for a
book, which lies on the floor.

"You would follow any woman." She pinches his
forearm.

"Why do you say that?" He turns on the light.

"Because you like women so much." She squints at
the bare bulb.

"Most men like women, unless they like men, and,
even then, sometimes they like women." He opens
the book, taking out a bookmark showing a scene of
Mount Fuji, a purple ribbon tied through a hole
punched in one end.

"But you like women more than most men. I
watch you and I can tell." As she lies on her side, she
holds the blanket to her chest, not looking at him.
"You like Hildy, don't you?"

He squeezes her neck, then begins to run his finger
down the notches of her spine.

"Rafael is coming back tomorrow."

80

"You've been telling me for weeks." He continues to caress her.

"I can't see you when he's back." The edges of the blanket's satin binding are frayed. She tries to break a loose thread, but it keeps unraveling.

"You were wearing black underwear tonight. Was that for me?" He kisses her shoulder, his lips soft, stubble scraping her skin.

"You never told me you liked such silly things." She kisses his shoulder in return. "What are you reading?"

"A story. . . . You must have known to wear them the last night we are together." He turns a page.

"I had no idea."

"If I fall while dancing, it becomes part of the performance. If your underwear is black, . . ."

"Happy accident."

She picks up the black underpants from the floor and tosses them onto the laundry pile. She changes the sheets, makes the bed, and, taking the ashtray from the coffee table, dumps the butts and ashes into the garbage. The breakfast dishes are not washed. Soseki left hours ago.

She clears the table, putting the dirty cups and saucers in the sink. She shakes the tea leaves from the pot and rinses it out. As she waits for the dishpan to fill with water, she stares at the building across the alley. The girl who lives there stands at her window,

81

watering plants. She is naked and seems to be watching Mara too. The girl waves, then lifts the old-fashioned watering can, as if in a toast. Startled, Mara tries to concentrate on scrubbing a plate. She waits a few minutes before raising her eyes to the window again. The girl is gone.

A streak of sunlight comes in from the west, halving the space diagonally. Mara sits on the couch, trying to decide what to wear. She wants to look radiant, although she does not feel so.

Having chosen a gray-blue dress, she puts it on over her head, then stands before the mirror. She raises her arms, stretching them out perpendicular to her body. The sleeves are wide, the dress straight and loose, like a kimono, but closed in front. The cloth is iridescent, shifting between gray and blue as she moves. She picks a red-lacquered chopstick from the jar and, without looking in the mirror, winds her hair in a knot, pushing the stick through the bun to keep it in place.

She waits by the customs gate, listening to the arrival of Rafael's flight announced over the loudspeaker. The doors open. A man, escorted by two policemen, is the first to come out. He does not look up.

Rafael calls out to her. His skin is brown, dark against the white shirt that he bought in Tonala.

Since she saw him last, his hair has grown longer and shaggier.

"You decided to come." He hugs her.

"I told you I would." She lets go of him, tries to pull away. "Do you have any other baggage?" She glances at the canvas duffle bag beside him.

Smiling, he shakes his head. "You look very good."

They walk out to the taxi stand. In the dark, they kiss, awkwardly, as if they do not know each other.

The taxi whizzes by a cluster of high-rise, brick apartment buildings. Rafael is kissing her like a thirsty dog lapping water. His eyes are shut, so he cannot see that she is staring out the window. She realizes that her dress is around her waist, wonders whether the cabdriver is watching them in his rear-view mirror.

Rafael pushes her down on the seat. Her head bangs against the ashtray on the car door; the chopstick snaps; her hair is shaken loose. Rafael bites her neck hard.

Her tights are down to her knees. The driver seems oblivious as he speeds through traffic.

"Rafael, we'll be home soon." She shoves him away from her.

He stops. She pulls her tights up, her dress down, and crosses her legs.

83

Reaching under her skirt, he puts his hand on her thigh.

They get out at Broadway. When Mara gives the cabdriver a twenty, he smirks at her.

"Do you think he was watching us?" she asks Rafael, as they walk up the stairs.

"I don't care. Does it matter to you?"

"A little. I like to do things in private." She ducks her head.

At the top of the second flight of stairs, he fumbles in his pocket.

"Your key won't work. I had a new lock put in while you were gone."

He seems surprised. "You didn't tell me—what happened?"

"The old one didn't work right. A couple of times I came home and couldn't get the door open." She turns the key.

"What did you do?" He goes in first, as she holds the door for him.

"I had to call the locksmith."

He looks around. "I can't take Mexico anymore. I feel crazy there. New York is the only place I can live."

"That's what you said in your letter. You never feel crazy here?" She pushes his hair from his forehead.

"I'm crazy everywhere." He laughs. "Is there anything to eat?" He goes to the refrigerator.

Putting her arms around his waist, she leans over his shoulder. "Bread, cheese—Guinness. Did you drink a lot after I left?"

"Enough tequila to fill a bathtub." He flips off the bottlecap.

"Do you want a glass for your beer?"

"No, *mamacita*." He takes a drink from the bottle.

She drains a jar of olives in the sink and pours them into a bowl. "How's your mother?"

"The same. She never changes."

"No, I mean how is she feeling since the operation."

"She complains, but she always complains."

"And Ascencio?"

"He got Bellas Artes to show his Times Square film."

"He keeps on showing the same thing." She puts the cheese on a board and slices some bread.

The subway passes underneath, causing the building to tremble. Hanging on chains from the ceiling, the fluorescent lights sway. Outside, a car rattles over the pavement.

He gets up and turns on the radio, fiddling with the dial.

La cumbia! El ritmo colombiano!

She does a couple of dance steps. "We never went to a cabaret in Mexico. Why was everyone afraid to go?"

"It's not a place to bring women. Everyone tries to

85

pick them up. Guys get into fights. There's always trouble."

Cumbia de la medianoche, cumbia de la madrugada.

"What is *la madrugada?*"

"Dawn, daybreak."

"How lovely to cumbia at dawn."

Standing, her back to the table, she watches him coming toward her.

He presses her against the table's edge, shoving his knee between hers, and lifts her onto the table top. She wraps one leg around his waist, supporting herself with her arm, holding his chin in her hand. Slowly, she undoes his belt.

"Always so careful," he whispers, unzipping quickly.

She crooks her other leg around his neck.

His hands underneath her, he raises her hips slightly. Her back bangs on the wood. The buttons on Rafael's shirt hurt her ribs, and his bony pelvis knocks against her. She tries to hold him still, but he does not stop moving. Digging her nails into his skin, she scratches his arms. He grimaces, looking ugly. As she averts her eyes, she bites his shoulder until he cries out. He grabs her hair, holding her head so that she cannot reach him with her mouth, then, raising himself, rolls her over onto her stomach. Something clatters to the floor. She can no longer see his face, but she now feels his breath on the back of her neck, hears it hissing behind her ear. He isn't hurting her, but she screams.

86

THE GARDEN

The old woman lifts the metal rack covering the basket. The turtles shift. One scrambles over the others, then butts against the wicker sides of the container. She reaches down and picks up a large turtle, which withdraws its head and tail, its fat, spotted limbs. She turns the reptile over and examines it, an orange mandala pattern on the belly, uses this one to poke the others, then drops it carelessly back into the basket.

The lobsters sit in a tray packed with shaved ice. Their backs are dark-bluish green, brighter at the joints, lace-edged fantails, large marine insects. The bigger ones have wide, beige rubber bands around their closed claws.

"What about lobster?" says Rafael.

"I've never cooked lobster." Mara sets her shopping bag on the sidewalk.

"You've never cooked crab either."

"But I've watched my father cook it many times. You just throw it into boiling water. Sometimes he used a can of beer instead, put some mustard in and a bay leaf. He would make a hot sauce to go with it, or garlic and butter."

The crabs are piled in an open basket. She chooses one, carefully holding its back legs. The shell is blue, limbs flecked with coral. The crab snaps its pincers at her. She asks the stall keeper for a bag. "How many should we get?"

"Who's coming?"

"Hildy is bringing someone. I'll get six?"

The old woman seems to have decided on two small turtles. Placing them on the rack, she argues the price with the stall keeper.

"Will you carry them?" Mara hands the crabs to Rafael.

"Someone's calling from outside. It must be Hildy." Mara removes the cover from the pot. Small bubbles appear; the water has begun to boil. "Would you go down and let her in?"

Rafael stands at the window. "She's with some Chinese guy. Her new lover?"

Mara takes a bottle of white wine from the refrigerator, sets out four glasses. The downstairs door slams. Voices come up the stairs, Hildy's above the others. The front door opens. The lock clicks. Mara wipes her hands on a paper towel.

Hildy is dressed in a black kimono printed with cranes in flight, her narrow eyes outlined in black. Mara offers her cheek to Hildy, but does not kiss her. She does the same with Soseki. His skin is cold, his scent familiar, disturbing, reminding her of bamboo mats. "How are you?" She shakes his hand, does not hear his answer. Holding Rafael's arm, she introduces him to Soseki.

Hildy seems surprised. "I thought you knew each other."

"Maybe we have met before." Soseki appears to scrutinize Rafael's features, then exclaims, "You look very familiar. In fact, you look Japanese."

"In fact, I am Japanese." Rafael grins.

Hildy takes a bottle from a paper bag. "We brought saki."

"Shall I heat some now? I just opened some white wine."

Hildy glances at Soseki. "We'll have wine."

"These paintings on the walls are yours?" Soseki asks Rafael.

"These are only a few of my pieces."

"Where are the others?"

"Some old ones are in Mexico, but I have many stored here."

"Rafael loves to show his paintings." Hildy winks at Mara.

"I would like to see them." Soseki follows Rafael to the other end of the space.

"They're not moving." Mara pokes a wooden spoon into the bucket. One crab snatches at it.

"You'll see how they struggle when you're about to pop them into hot water." Hildy passes her the tongs.

"I'm afraid it's going to turn around and pinch me, or grab my sleeve."

"Choose a quiet one."

Only one crab, standing on the others, its back a deeper blue, almost navy, clicking its pincers, seems to be alive.

Hildy extends her leg and pulls up the sagging ankle of her black tights.

Mara hesitates, then reaches the tongs to a motionless crab. The lively one, though, seizes the end of the utensil. She tries to shake it off, but it doesn't let go. Lifting the crab from the bucket, keeping it at arm's length, she steps toward the stove. Before reaching the pot, the crab falls to the floor and scuttles behind the refrigerator.

"I'll put the others in, while you try to get that one back." Hildy takes the tongs.

With a broomstick, Mara feels along the baseboard behind the refrigerator. As she touches something brittle, she shudders and withdraws the broom handle.

"Instead of mice, you'll have crabs scooting around your kitchen." Hildy replaces the lid on the pot. "Five minutes."

Rafael has pulled out some of his big paintings, resting them against the window frames. Mara cannot distinguish between the two voices, only talk from laughter.

"I didn't know you were seeing Soseki." Mara folds the napkins diagonally.

Her friend crosses her legs, both women following the movement with their eyes. Hildy speaks softly. "I like him. He's so charming. Of course, he's too charming. I don't usually trust a man who's like that." She giggles, then cups her mouth with one hand and whispers, "But I have two other lovers. It's always like this—feast or famine. I'm feasting right now."

"How do you manage it?" Mara arranges the asparagus lengthwise on an oval platter. "I could never handle more than one man at a time."

Hildy puts her arms into her kimono sleeves. "I have a schedule." They both laugh.

The water is boiling over. Mara lowers the flame. The crabs have turned an angry red, their claws remain tinged blue. "Could any still be alive?"

"They can't survive cooking." Hildy skims off

91

some of the light foam floating on top of the water, blows on it, then licks the spoon. "You should add this to the garlic and butter sauce."

Mara clears away the cheese, but leaves the French bread on the table. She drains the small, russet potatoes, steam burning her fingers.

Hildy opens the cupboard. "Where are the bowls for the sauce?"

Sitting across from Mara, Soseki strokes the stem of his glass. "All the paintings show skulls and women."

"The Mexican obsessions." Hildy pours butter sauce onto her plate. "Sex and death."

"What else is there?" Rafael runs his fingers through his hair.

"This crab is wonderful, sweeter than the ones we had last week," Hildy says to Soseki.

"You had them in a restaurant?" Mara unfolds her napkin, drops it on the floor, where it falls into a white peak.

"Soseki's friends gave a party. They're a troop that perform with live crabs, which they cook after the performance."

Rafael's head is bent over his crab. Breaking it open, he lays the two halves of the shell on his plate. The exposed meat is white, faintly pink around the edges. "Mara, didn't you describe something like that—you saw it while I was gone?"

"You're from Mexico, but you look Japanese."
With his fork, Soseki works on removing a piece of
crab from a curve in the shell.

"Other people say that. They think I'm from everywhere but Mexico. France, Greece, Italy, sometimes the Middle East. Once, this woman began to
speak to me in Russian because she thought she had
met me at a party in Moscow." He snaps off a claw.

Some men have beautiful hands, but Rafael's are
thick, stubby-fingered, as if someone has lopped off
the first joint. He twists one leg from the body,
bending it back to get inside. Cracking the limb between his teeth, he sucks out the meat.

"People always mistake me for Japanese." Soseki
tilts the unbroken shell, extracting a sliver of crab.

"Have some asparagus." Mara passes the dish to
Soseki. She refills the wine glasses, but only halfway.

"Is there more wine?" Rafael looks at her sharply.

"Of course. Two other bottles, and Soseki and
Hildy brought saki."

"Mara always forgets things," he explains. "Nothing is worse than to run out of wine during dinner."

The plates are heaped with split claws and scraped
shells. Two slender asparagus spears lie in greenish
water at the bottom of the dish. The potatoes have
been eaten. "The salad." Mara jumps up.

"And the rest of the crabs?" Rafael empties the
wine bottle into his glass.

93

"There's one more. The three of you can divide it."

"Why don't you sit down and eat. You haven't touched your food." Hildy slides out of her chair. "I'll get the salad and serve the crab."

"Don't you like it?" Rafael's fork clatters against his plate.

"I'm just not hungry." Mara tries to smile. "Rafael, why don't you have mine, and Soseki and Hildy will divide the other one."

"I thought you bought six?"

"One escaped." She changes plates with him.

Hildy sets out the salad—spinach, shredded violet cabbage, quartered tomatoes, thin circles of radish, grated carrots, some black olives.

Soseki says something about the colors. His voice fades. Mara inclines her head toward him to hear better, looking past him to the street, hazy pink from the lights, the loft across the alley dark. Intermittent whines of an ambulance siren peak, then dim, and die away.

Hildy dips a piece of bread into the hot sauce. "Coriander?"

"Yes, it's a Mexican *salsa picante*. Rafael made it— fried *chiles,* tomato, coriander. If you don't care for it, use the garlic sauce."

"It's . . . interesting." Hildy laughs, arches a thin eyebrow at Rafael.

"I thought you liked things hot." Rafael wipes his mouth on his sleeve.

94

"He ground the *chile* on his grandmother's *molcajete.*"

Soseki asks what is a *molcajete.*

"A sort of mortar for grinding." Mara runs her fingers over the faggoting in the tablecloth. "Rafael's is basalt."

"We use it for making sauces, grinding *chiles.* This one belonged to my grandmother, who was young during the Revolution. Her mother gave it to her when she was married. It has a chip on one side from when my grandfather threw it at her."

"Why did he do that?" Hildy picks an olive out of the salad.

"He was a very jealous man, ten years older than she was and always watching her. One day he went with my grandmother, her sister, and some of the children to the country. They met some *charros* who were drinking and playing the guitar, having a party—"

Hildy interrupts. "What are *charros?*"

"Mexican cowboys. The ones from Jalisco are famous. They're considered sort of aristocrats. Gentlemen ranchers." Mara looks at Rafael.

He nods and continues. "The *charros* invited them to drink tequila. My grandmother was a very pretty woman, friendly, always joking. Well, one *charro* asked her to dance and she did. My grandfather didn't wait for the music to finish. He grabbed her by the arm, told her not to dance with this man. The *charro* put his hand on his gun, and my grandfather was ready

95

to fight; but my grandmother and her sister pulled him away. That night, when they got home, my grandfather threw the *molcajete* at my grandmother. If he hadn't been drunk and missed, she might have been killed."

"Mara better watch her step with that kind of blood in the family." Hildy rests her arm on the back of her chair.

"If it had been a Japanese story, he would have killed his wife; and her ghost would have haunted him until he went mad." Soseki sips his wine, then lowers his head, as Hildy whispers something to him.

"Come on. No secrets." Rafael thumps the table with the flat of his hand, sloshing the wine in his glass.

"No secrets, Rafael. I was saying to Soseki that we should all go to the Ephesian Garden after dinner."

Rafael raises his glass. "They have wonderful girls there. Let's go. Let's drink to the girls."

"Do you mind if I have a cigarette?" Soseki asks Mara.

She sets an ashtray beside him. "Saki? Or I can make coffee?"

"We can drink there." Rafael stands up.

Hildy turns on the faucet. "I'll rinse off the plates. Why don't you get ready."

"I really don't know if I should go. It's late. If Rafael wants to go with you . . ." Mara wipes her forehead with the back of her hand.

THE GARDEN

"I want you to come." Rafael tries to get his arm into the sleeve of his overcoat, but misses.

Smoke floats upward, hiding Soseki's face.

Something moves across the floor. A crab hurries along the wall, then disappears under the sofa.

The entrance to the Ephesian Garden, an unobtrusive doorway on the ground floor of an old brick tenement on West Twenty-ninth Street, has no sign. They pass through a small, tiled hallway, blue rosettes on the floor, a red meander along the wall.

The inside of the club is dark, lit by candles flickering in cut glass tumblers on the tables and lamps mounted on wall brackets, which illuminate a mural of women reclining under palm trees and beside fountains, a caravan painted in the background.

A waiter in a red jacket shows them to a table fronting a small oval dance floor, behind which is a low stage. A bouzouki player, an accordionist, a guitarist, and a violinist—all men—and a woman with bleached hair, who is singing plaintively, sit in café chairs on the stage, a microphone before each one. The performers, blank-faced except for the singer, whose black eyebrows scowl at the audience, are stiff, their backs straight. Only the musicians' hands move. The music softens. The woman rises, removes the microphone from the stand, whipping the cord across the floor. She speaks with an accent, her voice deep and raspy. "Gentlemen and ladies, it's a pleasure to have with us tonight—Bobbie of Istanbul!" She mimes applause. The waiters and customers clap haphazardly.

At the next table, two middle-aged men in light-colored suits, dark shirts, and wide ties sit with a young girl, her bangs over smudged eyes. One of the men, who is bald, lifting his arms above his head, applauds to the rhythm.

The singer nods to the musicians. The bouzouki player picks a few high notes, followed by a flutter of lower ones.

A waiter sets down a plate of feta, peppers, and olives. Rafael, holding himself, hands under his armpits, asks for a bottle of retsina. He slices a pepper, scraping out the seeds.

Clanging finger cymbals, Bobbie of Istanbul enters from the back of the club. Her veils brush Mara's hands as she passes their table. Each step is accentuated by a shake of her hips. Her back is plump, flesh indented by the straps of her gold brassiere. The coins on her costume jangle like change in a pocket. With a swish of her yellow skirt, she spins around. Her navel, deep as a bullet hole, sinks into her soft belly.

"There's so much of her," Mara whispers.

"In the old days, a dancer was supposed to be able to hold a cup of oil in her navel." Hildy takes a drag from Soseki's cigarette.

The dancer circles the floor with measured steps.

Her shoulders quiver, the sequins casting spots of light across the ceiling. Independent of the rest of her body, her stomach rotates under the skin. She throws her head back, hair sweeping over her face, hips switching like an accelerated pendulum, coins jingling in counterpoint to the cymbals.

As the rhythm of the music becomes faster, she whirls into a series of turns, her skirt fanning out, a blur of sequins and yellow cloth.

The unaccompanied bouzouki repeats the melody, this time slow and insistent. Bobbie dances before the girl and the two men. She drops into a deep knee bend. The bald man opens his wallet and stuffs a bill between her breasts. The coins clink louder.

Shaking her red hair, damp tendrils clinging to her temples, she approaches Mara's table. Bobbie licks her lips, her tongue violet under the spotlights. Her metallic fringe is close to Rafael's face, a brown areola showing. He wipes the corner of his mouth. Reaching deep into his pocket, he takes out a handful of bills. She jerks her hips emphatically. He folds one and carefully tucks it into the band of her lower costume—on the right side—then another on the left, and, digging his fingers down, a third in the center. She clangs her cymbals, spins around, swiveling her dimpled haunches. He goes into his pants again, rolling what looks like a ten, and shoves it into the crack.

"You've never given the dancer money before."

Mara stares at an artificial grapevine spiraling the column behind Rafael's head.

He orders a second bottle of retsina. His eyes seem to follow Bobbie as she snakes past the men along the bar.

The bald man in the light suit, cheered on by the other man and the girl, stands in the center of the floor, his shoulders hunched, eyes closed, then starts a series of slow steps, moving in a semicircle. He takes out a handkerchief, drops it on the floor, and begins to dance around it. The men in the audience yell encouragement. A waiter rushes up and showers him with dollar bills. The other man shouts something from his seat.

Half rising from his chair, Rafael calls, "Retsina, retsina! Bring him a bottle of retsina!"

Hildy stands up, quickly taking Soseki's hand. "Come on, Mara. Dance with us."

She follows them onto the floor, where she joins hands with Soseki. His palm is dry. Her fingers keep slipping out of his. She hears the violin, as though a heavy curtain were separating her from the sound of the instrument. His steps criss-crossing, the bald man reaches for Hildy and leads them into a dance. He makes a sudden turn and jerks Hildy from Soseki.

No longer imitating the other man, Soseki puts his arms around Mara and guides her through an exaggerated tango, bending her over his knee. She lifts her leg

100

to keep balance. Pressing her hand, he twines his fingers with hers, then pulls her up and starts to waltz.

Over Soseki's shoulder, she sees Rafael staring at them, a glass to his mouth. Head cocked to one side, Soseki twirls her around. His arms are raised, elbows bent; he is doing something fancy with his feet, rocking from one side to the other. Every few beats, he lifts the same foot twice. He jumps higher, both hands about her waist, carrying her up with him, holding her, it seems, in midair. Under the spotlights, his teeth and the whites of his eyes appear fluorescent blue. The singer wails, carrying the note, dipping it into the lower range, then drawing it up and extending the sound into a cry.

Something small strikes Mara's cheek. She stumbles. Soseki steadies her. She looks at Rafael, who is standing, arm raised. Pennies and silver change roll under her feet. She runs toward him.

A big man in an open shirt and a tight sports jacket pushes a chair aside. "Say, fella, you don't throw things around in this place, not at a customer, even if she's your girlfriend."

"Listen, man." Rafael sounds as if he is trying to speak very carefully. "People give money to the dancers here. I ran out of dollars, so I give my change."

"Don't get wise with me." The man chews one side

101

of his lip. "Lady, take your boyfriend somewhere else. We don't wanna have any trouble around here."

"We're leaving." Mara picks up Rafael's overcoat.

"But I ordered another bottle of wine." He waves to the waiter.

"Pay your check and take it with you."

They stand on the corner of Eighth Avenue and Twenty-ninth Street. Hildy's fur collar is turned up, covering the lower part of her face. She passes a lighted cigarette to Soseki. No one speaks. Mara, her arm around Rafael's waist, can feel his body swaying.

"The dinner was very good." Soseki holds out his hand. Mara shakes it. He turns to Rafael, who stares at him as if he does not understand the gesture. Soseki shrugs.

Mara presses her cheek to Hildy's. Neither kisses the other.

"The crab was lovely. Let's get together soon."

"Yes. Let's."

Hildy pats Rafael's hand. "Lay off the retsina—Oh, there's a cab. We better grab it. See you."

Rafael leans against a building. "She's a *puta,* a whore."

"What do you mean?"

"She's your friend, but she always tries to fuck me."

"When has she tried?"

"When you were visiting your parents, she invited me to dinner." He pauses. "But all women are whores."

"She was just being nice."

He steps away from the wall. "I don't want to know your fucking lovers! But I know you—you go around trying to tie up every guy you meet. I'm not stupid. I can see what's going on with this guy. *Puta madre!*" He glares at her, then grabs a garbage can and throws it against the concrete, cursing loudly in Spanish. The lid rolls off the curb, down the dark street, like a pitched nickel, then hits something, falling over in a series of clangs. "You don't want to fuck with me, so I'm like a burro on a rope. But you're screwing around, shaking your ass every place you go. I don't care who you fuck, I'm not going to fight over you. I don't fight over a woman."

"You don't have to fight over me—I'm not with anyone but you. Why do you call me a whore?" She spits.

He slaps her, a sharp crack across the cheek.

They walk downtown on Eighth Avenue, not together, but parallel to each other, Mara along the curb, Rafael close to the buildings. Her heel catches in a subway grate. She does not trip, but steps out of her shoe. As she stops to put it back on, she sees him continue. He seems to speed up; then he turns down a side street. In a minute, her shoe on, she hurries after him. When she reaches the corner, she looks down both sides of the block, but does not see anyone.

The sky is pink in the east as she crosses the paved drive just off La Guardia Place. The modern apartment houses surround a grassy plot, its north end marked by a vertical-seeming concrete sculpture, about three or four stories high, which, as she approaches, unfolds into a monumental bust of a woman, a series of planes placed at different angles, the features and hair drawn in dark streaks over the surface. At the base, nestled in the vertex of two planes, a man, thin and dark, slouches, one knee raised, foot resting on the concrete. She runs over the wet lawn toward him, but when she reaches the monument, he is no longer there. She goes around to the other side and discovers another face on the back of the sculpture, but the man has disappeared.

As Mara enters the loft, she hears dripping. She remains still for a moment, trying to determine the sound's location, decides the bathroom.

The door is ajar, the light on. Holding the knob, she pushes it open. Shirtless, his back toward her,

Rafael is standing on a white towel before the toilet. His belt hangs loose at the hip. He is breathing hard.

"Rafael?" She unbuttons her coat, places it over the edge of the bathtub.

He does not turn around.

Slipping off her shoes, she walks up behind him. With the tip of her tongue, she touches the vaccination scar on his shoulder. "Let me do it for you?"

His arm drops to his side.

She kneels down.

THE RECITAL

The tall windows are covered with heavy velvet curtains, drawn so that all the light in the room comes from the glass chandelier in the center of the high, coffered ceiling. Two paintings—a doughy-faced Virgin holding a cheerful infant on her knees and a horseman, red-coated and heroic (maybe Simón Bolívar)—hang on opposite walls. While Ascencio fusses with cords, Rafael loads film into the camera.

"Put the lights around the center. That's where Escolar will sit." Wearing a gray sweat shirt, sleeves pushed up, and black, wraparound sunglasses, Ascencio directs Rafael.

Rafael sets up the lights around the table area. He kneels on the floor as he adjusts the heights of the stands. Licking his lips, he grins shyly at Mara, who is at the end of the table near the door, then glances around as if to see whether anyone has noticed. He will hold the camera. Ascencio will do the sound.

A tall middle-aged woman in a beige suit enters. Gesturing toward the chair next to Mara, she asks, "Is anyone sitting here?" Her face is tight and tanned, her lips greasy pink. Mara scowls and shakes her head. The woman sits down and starts searching through her purse. Taking a cigarette from a leather case, she lights it, blowing smoke in Mara's direction.

Rafael takes off his sweater and hands it to Mara to hold for him. The woman next to her stares at him, as she taps the table with her glossy fingernails, which click annoyingly against the wood.

About a dozen people are around the table, all of them well-dressed and important-looking. One seat in the middle is still empty. Apparently, Escolar has not yet arrived. His translator, Alberto Lanciani, who will act as moderator, stands by, rubbing the tip of his nose and peering anxiously through thick glasses at the audience. With the camera on his shoulder, Rafael aims at Escolar's vacant chair.

She hears the bathroom door open. He hesitates, holding the camera before him. She watches as he

107

puts it on the floor and, stepping out of his clothes, steps into the tub, splashing water as he gets in.

I'm not quite the fool that people admire me for being.

Mara opens her eyes. An old man is sitting in Escolar's place. Speaking quietly, he turns his head, as if to address Mara's side of the table. One of his eyelids droops, while the other is unnaturally taut, the eye beneath wide and staring. The audience laughs politely, and Ascencio, who holds the microphone, nods graciously, as if he himself has spoken.

"Although this may disappoint some of my readers who have obtained some pleasure from my departure from the real, the provincial, the petty, the stupidly cruel, who like to remind themselves that I have, as they say, spent the better part of my adult life in the Buenos Aires Public Library and that I have avoided people in order to live amongst books, I am rewriting my earlier stories that were, in the words of Mr. Dew-Matthews, 'a venturesome solace from the commonplace, from fear of normal social activity, from fear itself.'" Escolar pauses to cough into his handkerchief.

He takes the camera from the floor and sets it on her stomach, the lens toward the upper part of her body. He snaps the shutter. "Is it all right if it gets wet?" she asks in a small voice.

108

Rafael has changed position and is leaning against a window frame. Although he faces Mara, he does not look at her; instead, he seems to be staring at the woman in the beige suit. From across the room, however, his eyes are blurred, and Mara is not sure whom he is watching. When he lowers the camera momentarily, he sticks out his tongue.

"Insolent bastard!" someone mutters close by.

Mara turns indignantly to the woman next to her, only to see her smiling calmly.

She sits up suddenly, and the camera slips into the bathwater. She lifts it out, dries it off with a towel, and aims it at him, as he crouches at the other end of the tub, hiding his eyes with his arm.

Leaning over to whisper something to his translator, Escolar sips water from the glass in front of him. "As you may know, I am blind; therefore, it is impossible for me to give a reading. I have, however, committed to memory a great many of my works, both in their original Spanish and in English translation. Mr. Lanciani will follow along with the text and supply the words if my memory fails me. I will repeat a story that is itself a reworking of 'Cesc Gallango,' which I wrote in 1934." The writer sinks back into his chair and puts his hands together, his fingertips touching each other. Ascencio hovers behind him, his dark glasses showing directly above Escolar's head, so that the old man appears to have a double forehead. His drooping eyelid falls even lower, almost covering the eye below it.

"It was August in the summer of 1893 when I first observed Gallango's bookstore on the corner of Avenida de La Paz in the old section of the city. The sun was very strong that day; and, noticing the dark, cool-looking shop, with old, leather-bound volumes and maps in the window, I tapped on the door. I stood there waiting for a few minutes and, thinking that it must be closed after all, turned to leave when a sallow-skinned man came to the door and, after sizing me up, removed the latch, allowing me to enter."

Taking a few long steps from the window, Rafael again faces Escolar. He turns the lens toward Mara. The woman in the beige suit hooks her finger into the strand of pearls around her neck, as she looks directly into the camera. Rafael winks at them. The woman throws back her head and laughs shrilly. No one seems disturbed by the noise. Escolar continues to speak in a low, even voice. The laughter stops.

She stands up, the water up to her calves. He lowers his arm a little, then covers his eyes again, flattening out his nose. His lips move; he whispers in Spanish. The vaccination mark on his shoulder is puckered from the bath. Holding the camera in one hand, she pries his arm away from his face with the other. Now quiet, he stops resisting. His arms fall to his sides, his hands under the water, fingers splayed and greenish. Bending, she reaches for his hand. Drawing it out, she puts it to her cheek, feeling the hairs on the back of his hand. She turns it over and presses her face into his wet palm, her eyes tightly shut. His fingers close around the edges of her face. Letting the camera go, she leans clumsily against him.

Mara slumps in her chair. Escolar's voice has become very loud, as if he were shouting into a microphone. She claps her hands over her ears and cannot hear anything. Escolar's mouth continues to move. Rafael and Ascencio change places very quickly. Lifting two fingers to see if Escolar is still bellowing, Mara hears nothing but a whirring sound that seems to come from inside her head. His mouth opening and closing silently, Escolar looks like a fish breathing. She holds onto the armrests of her chair and waits, hoping that no one will notice her. Yet it seems as if everyone in the room is staring in her direction. A man with short, black hair turns his head to look at her, casually flicking the ashes from his cigarette into the ashtray before him.

Mara feels as cold as if she were naked. She shuts her eyes. Her head buzzes but the room is silent. She does not move.

THE OTHER SIDE

At night the windows let people outside see in. Mara turns off the lights, so that no one can watch her from the street or from the buildings nearby.

She lies in the dark, filling in the shadows of the table, the chairs, the desk, imagining them in daylight. From the couch, she can see the entire space except the far corner where Rafael's easel stands, which is blocked by the closet built between the first and second windows. The view of the skyscraper across the street is broken by a row of paintings stored in the space between the makeshift and structural walls. The paintings resemble enormous books, all narrow-spined, but of different heights. The street

112

lamps and the moonlight make her hands look
wrinkled, her bare, stretched out legs withered, the
skin pale and mottled. She reaches for the switch of
the standing lamp beside the couch. After two clicks,
one of the bulbs lights up, returning both the room
and her body to their usual appearance.

She hears voices from next door. The wall between
the two spaces is thin. She listens to a man and a
woman talking.

They were married that summer.

I remember she wore a yellow dress, a short one.

Her mother thought it should be white.

*She carried a bouquet of roses of different colors. She said
they scratched her arms.*

*She stood in a corner talking to him, as though nobody
else were there.*

*The veil covered her face. She put her hand to her mouth
when she laughed.*

She always did that.

They were old friends?

Her mother never liked him.

His profession, maybe?

He was in the theater.

An actor?

He acted like an actor.

Why did she go into the garden?

*Someone remembered her saying that she wanted to see the
poppies in bloom.*

They saw her with him?

She came back later, leaning on his arm.
She explained it?
She said the sun was very strong, so she was sitting in the gazebo, where she fell asleep. He found her there and brought her back.
How long was she gone?
Hours.

Mara drops one leg to the floor, then the other. She sits up, shakes her head, trying to clear it. Stepping into her slippers, she ties the belt of her cotton robe, rolls up the sleeves. From the chest, she takes a clean towel and washcloth, then opens the bathroom door.

A blond girl, maybe thirteen or fourteen, is sitting in the tub. Her breasts are childish, her shoulders narrow. A man is watching her, his back toward Mara. He holds something in front of him. She can't make out what it is. As he puts it on the floor, Mara sees that it is a camera. He wears a shirt and slacks. With one movement of his hand, his clothes drop to the floor. The girl smiles, then covers her mouth with her hand. He gets in, displacing the water. Mara wipes her arm. The girl lifts her knees and hugs them to her, as if to protect her body. She is still smiling, but with a kind of curiosity or bewilderment. He tells her to put her legs down and lie back, as if she were in bed, which she does. Her nipples poke out of the water, the rest of her body submerged. He strad-dles her, then reaches for the camera and places it on

114

her belly. Her small face floats on the surface of the water, her hair swirling around it. He takes the picture. The girl says something that Mara cannot hear. He shakes his head, then bends down to kiss the girl's breasts, which he does quickly, not lingering. The girl pulls herself up, and the camera tumbles into the bath. She fishes it out and dries it with a towel. Head bowed, the girl slips the camera strap around her neck. As she looks at the man through the viewer, she pushes her wet hair away from her face. He is huddled on the other side, his arm over his eyes.

The camera in one hand, the girl grips the edge of the bathtub. She stands, swaybacked, her stomach pushed out, elbows bent behind her. She perches on the rim of the tub, her feet in water, the camera in her lap. Raising his arm, the man steals a look at her, then hides his face again.

With his eyes still covered, he throws his head over the side of the tub. Kneeling, the girl picks up his hand. As she holds it to her face, she rubs her cheek against it. Her expression serious, she looks toward Mara. With eyes closed, the girl rests her head in the man's palm. His other hand moves from the curve of the girl's back, notched down the center, to her shoulders and dripping hair. Scooping out water, he splashes the girl, who falls awkwardly into his arms.

Lifting herself out of the bath, Mara reaches for the towel hanging on a hook. She dries her neck and

115

chest first, then her back. The mirror is clouded with
steam. Again, the voices come through the wall.

He followed you all night.
He stood at my side.
What did he want?
He asked a lot of questions.
What did he want to know?
If I was alone.
What did you say?
That I was, but that you were here too.
*I was standing by the window, watching. You looked
around the room. I thought you saw me.*
I did. I wanted to make certain I wasn't lying.
Did you tell him?
Everything he wanted to know.
Then he left?
I went to find you.
Did you?
I opened the door and thought I saw you with her.
Was it me?
*It was a mistake, some other man. He didn't look any-
thing like you, I realized later.*
If it had been me, what would you have done?
I'm not sure—left maybe, left with him.

The telephone rings once. She walks slowly toward
the desk, picks up the receiver, presses it against her
ear.

116

"Hi." People are talking in the background.

"Hello. Where are you? It's so noisy." She folds back the cuff of her robe, then unfolds it.

"At a party. A Halloween party—*El Día de los Muertos.* You should come."

"Give me the address."

She pulls the string, turning on the bathroom light. The mirror is still patched with steam, which she wipes away with the heel of her hand. She powders her face, then outlines her mouth and eyes with red pencil, smudges gold and turquoise on her eyelids.

Pushing aside other clothes, she takes out the Chinese dress—pale yellow silk, a trellis of red roses embroidered diagonally from one shoulder to the opposite hip—and lays it on the bed. She pulls in her stomach as she zips the side zipper, swallows as she fastens the frogs at the neck. The high collar chokes her, so she undoes the hook and eye at the top. Although she has raised the slits, the dress is still too tight to take very big steps.

One by one, she removes the hairpins from her hair, which falls over one shoulder.

When she leaves, she checks to make sure that the stove is off, and that the telephone receiver is in its cradle.

The party is filled with women and smoke. A naked girl in high heels minces past, her shoulders

117

thrown back in an unnaturally erect posture, holding a champagne glass before her. From both sides, the guests push against Mara. She works her way past three ingénues in short skirts, stepping on their toes as she does. Seeming not to notice, they continue their conversation. Mara catches the word *mascara* repeated several times, takes a second look at them, noticing their square jaws, muscular arms, large hands.

The music is loud, its rhythm compulsive.

Do it, do it—whatever it is—do it 'til you're satisfied.

Someone taps Mara's shoulder. She turns around. A man with rouged cheeks and a beard, in a pink tutu, tights and satin slippers, waves a wand topped with a silver paper star. "Make a wish." He winks at her.

As she moves away from the man with the wand, a black woman, over six feet tall, in a purple Cleopatra wig and mauve furs, smiles down at her. "You lost, honey?"

"I'm looking for someone." Mara does not want to say her husband.

"I'm Candy Cane Hooker, John Lee's daughter, and maybe I can help you."

"I'm sure I'll find him." Mara thanks Candy Cane and pushes on.

Do it slow . . . whatever it is . . . Do it 'til you're satisfied. . . . I'm satisfied, I'm satisfied . . . The falsetto dies away.

Drums and shouts. The music turns Brazilian. A

118

woman in a silver jump suit and helmet begins to samba, her hips and shoulders swaying back and forth as she advances, fists clenched. Other dancers line up behind her, all holding each other's waists, following her, starting and stopping with the music. The woman in silver leads the line around Mara. The dancers drop hands and begin to clap, the circle closing in on her. The lights go out. A strobe light flashes on, momentarily fixing the movements of the dancers. It blinks faster and faster, the spiral of bodies a pulse of feathers, skin, teeth.

"Mara!" Someone grabs her hand, draws her from the dancers, breaking the line.

Hildy's face is half-hidden by a black domino. Her lips are red. She holds a long cigarette in her gloved hand.

"I'm looking for Rafael. Have you seen him?"

Hildy squeezes her hand, whispers, "Yes, he's here. But before you go to him, you must eat and drink."

Mara follows, as Hildy threads a way through the party.

At the other end of the room, a long table runs the length of the wall. People are moving slowly, loading plates and filling glasses. Smiling girls in tuxedo leotards and fish-net stockings ladle out punch from a bathtub-sized glass bowl. Further on, platters are heaped with pastries, tarts, cakes, chocolates, fruit of all kinds, nuts, black and red caviar, wheels of

119

cheese, baskets of bread, slices of cold meat, ham, lamb, stuffed turkey, duck, pheasant.

"And Rafael?" Mara nibbles an éclair.

Hildy lifts her mask for a moment, lowers it quickly. "Wait a few minutes more."

Mara wraps her pastry in a napkin, which she sets down on the edge of the table between a Sacher torte, which looks as if pieces have been torn out by hand, and a vase of long-stemmed tiger lilies. She loosens another hook at the neck of her dress, breathes deeply. Breaking off a lily, she tucks it behind her ear.

"Now." Hildy points with her gloved finger to a doorway. "Down the hall, the last door on the left." She kisses Mara on both cheeks, laughs softly as she wipes the lipstick mark away.

As Mara walks down the hall, the music grows softer. The walls are white, the rug gray, fluorescent lights above. She passes many doors on both sides. Stopping, she tries one, but it is locked. A telephone on the wall is ringing. She answers it. Two men are talking in a language that she does not recognize. She listens for a minute to see if she can understand anything, cannot, hangs up. The telephone continues to ring, although the sound becomes fainter as she walks away. Ahead, the hallway curves, so that she cannot see more than a few yards before her. The rug seems to be growing deeper. Her heels sink into it. Without her noticing, the walls have turned a dove-gray. The hallway ends in a point, a door on each side. She remembers that Hildy said left.

Since there is no knob or handle, she pushes the door, which opens. The room is glaringly bright, completely white, without furniture, bare walls, silent, empty—but for Rafael and a blond woman dancing. Her pale arms are around his neck, white fingers in his black hair, her head at an angle as they kiss. A wide-brimmed black hat hides his eyes. His hands are lost in her white skirts. The woman pulls away from him, looks directly at Mara. Her sad eyes are disdainful. The two figures move apart, but not quickly. Rafael does not seem to see Mara, yet he steps backward.

Mara reaches out and grabs the woman by the hair, jerking her head back. Mara feels her own dress rip. The flower falls from her hair. The soft face gives way under her fingers. The woman collapses onto the floor. Mara hears a voice. Her own or the other woman's—she is not sure.

THE PROOF

The lamp is still on. She has been sleeping on a nest of hairpins. Her socks and shoes are still on.

She slept against the wall for years. Now she sleeps in the middle of the mattress.

She doesn't bother to make the bed anymore.

When he was there, she never swept, still doesn't.

He always cooked. Now she eats sandwiches.

She puts up a new shower curtain, orange, like the robe of a Buddhist monk, but plastic.

She buys a shopping cart.

He said take everything you want.
He didn't want anything.

122

Nothing was his, he said.

He left a palette with paint still on it, bits of charcoal, brushes in turpentine, some loose razor blades.

He said she should ask Ascencio to help her if she wanted to move things around.

She hangs keys, pots and pans on the nails that are still in the walls.

Sometimes, she complains about him.

Remedios calls her up, crying. Mara doesn't understand what she is saying. They cry together.

She tries to clear the space, gives away the musty couch, the armchair, the big desk.

Every object reminds her of a particular moment or scene, some of several. She keeps giving things away.

She still buys cocoanut soap, even though it gives her a rash.

He said all the paintings are yours, if you want them. At first she refused them, then changed her mind. What else was there worth keeping?

She takes down all the paintings, turns them against the wall, avoids them. Sometimes, she looks through them—not at the paintings—reading the titles written on the backs of the stretchers.

Mara as an Eagle.

La Vaca Pendeja.

El Mosco.

Sometimes My Friend.

SPECTATOR

The Temple of 11,000 Virgins.
El Gusano Verde.
Mara with Chicken Legs.
Each painting is a story, but she is forgetting.

He asks her if she has hung the paintings.
She shrugs, you know how it is, later puts up
Mara as an Eagle.

Mara riffles through the photographs, finds one of
her and Rafael taken in Guadalajara.
Their figures stand out against a red curtain, half-
drawn. Her back toward the camera, she is playing a
bamboo flute. He watches the Mara in the photograph, while he holds another flute, which crosses
hers. His mouth is open, as if he is speaking. From
the window behind them, the sun throws a stroke of
light that falls on her left wrist, over her curved
knuckles.
They were happy that day.
Underneath, another picture, this one black and
white. They are wearing different clothes than in the
other photograph, but they are sitting before the
same window.
Something went wrong, for the print looks as if it
has exploded—a fuzzy streak runs from one corner to
the other, obliterating Rafael's face. Her own is quite
clear—her head tilted in a kiss, her eyes closed, her

124

arm around his neck. They must have loved each other then—there it is in the photograph.

She would like to show Rafael the picture. If he were here, he would see for himself. They did love each other. The photograph is proof.